# MOZART'S
# LAST
# WORDS

Other Works by Roy Ziegler

Novels
*Twilight of Separation*
*Dawn's Eerie Light*
*Requiem for Riley*

History
*New Hope, Pennsylvania: River Town Passages*
*The Parrys of Philadelphia and New Hope*
*Unfaltering Trust*

Children's Literature

*Let's Visit New Hope*
(Co-authored with Gayle Goodman and Pat Achilles)

# MOZART'S LAST WORDS

# ROY ZIEGLER

Library of Congress Control Number:      2022915613
ISBN:               Hardcover            978-1-6698-4384-9
                    Softcover            978-1-6698-4383-2
                    eBook                978-1-6698-4382-5

This is a work of historical fiction.

Print information available on the last page.

Rev. date: 10/25/2022

**To order additional copies of this book, contact:**
Xlibris
844-714-8691
www.Xlibris.com
Orders@Xlibris.com
846138

# Acknowledgements

*T*he author wishes to thank Charles F. Tarr, the City of Brussels, Archives Department, and the Austrian National Library for their assistance with the production of this book.

## SPECIAL ACKNOWLEDGEMENT TO

Bernard F. Stehle

*"Mozart's music is so pure and beautiful that I see it as a reflection of the inner beauty of the universe."*
– as recalled by Peter Bucky, *The Private Albert Einstein* (1933)

# Chapter 1

Chief Inspector Leopold Beckers leaned back in his office chair, couching the back of his head in his hands as he scanned the ghostly grey outlines on the empty wall across the room. Until two days earlier, it had displayed memorabilia highlighting his 45-year career with the Brussels Police Department. Recalling the certificate for the National Medal of Honor, and the photograph of himself with King Albert that had graced that wall for three decades, Leopold felt the widening bald spot on the top of his head—*Christ, did I ever really have all that hair?* He remembered posing for that picture with his military-style bearing. Glancing at his belly, he sighed. *Gravity! What can you do?*

The chief inspector signed the last of the documents on his desk and tossed it into the OUT basket. His retirement had finally come. But one case obsessed him to his final day on the job. Leaning sideways, he fished a ring of keys from his pocket, selected the smallest one, then grunted as he bent over to unlock the bottom right-hand drawer. Tugging at it, he finally forced open the warped oak receptacle. *Damned thing never worked from the day they delivered it!* He stared for a moment at the light-blue gusseted folder inside— the faded red "CASE CLOSED" rubber-stamped on the cover. Grasping it with both hands, he hoisted the file onto his desk. *There's no way I'm leaving this one behind!*

Officially ruling it a suicide, the department had closed the case twenty-five years earlier. But Beckers regretted that bureaucrats above his rank had failed to pursue the case with enough diligence, despite his repeated efforts over the years to keep it open. Unexplained circumstances surrounding the incident at the Atomium in Brussels on that torrid summer evening in 1990 remained unresolved. An American Vietnam War veteran lay sprawled on the floor, a gunshot to his head at close range, and a black CZ-70 firearm next to his body; bloody shoeprints tracked out to the iconic building's rear door, which had been forced open. A penknife was discovered ten feet from the corpse—its blade wide open, its pearl handle adorned with two ruby-encrusted crosses and the initials *CJL* engraved in 24-karat gold between the gems. All of this continued to haunt the old detective. *Screw the evidence records retention laws!*

Beckers lifted his time-worn leather briefcase to the top of the desk. After stuffing the file inside the case and tightening both tarnished brass buckles securely, he paused as he thought about his wife's smile when he opened it that first time—her gift celebrating his promotion to chief inspector. *God, I miss you, Elizabeth!* Leopold picked up the briefcase and walked to the door, hesitating for a moment after opening it. Turning around, he scanned the room that had defined his workdays for half a century. Then, one last time, he flicked out the lights and shut the door behind him.

Outside, Beckers' staff had formed a row on each side of the door, cheering as he emerged.

"Speech!" shouted his secretary, who, for thirty years, had unsuccessfully tried to organize Leopold's schedule. A dozen employees taunted him until Beckers set his briefcase on the floor and, raising both arms high in the air in surrender, obliged them.

"Well, I thought you had quite your fill of me at last night's dinner—thank you again for that unforgettable evening. ... Now, I know you all have a hell of a lot of work to do, especially in light of my imminent departure, so I won't keep you from your grave responsibilities."

The staff's catcalls rejected their chief's urging them to return to work.

"Seriously, though, and I know I am repeating myself, you all have been a top-notch team and I ... well ... you've made my job such a damned pleasure these many years—most of the time," he said. "And think about all those phenomenal cases we solved together!"

They applauded, cheering him again.

"I am heading to the states to visit my daughter in New York City, but, otherwise, I'm not going to be so far away that you won't be bumping into me at the local pubs and markets. Just keep doing the spectacular job you do."

He reached down and lifted his briefcase, took a deep breath, and walked down the faded marble hallway for the last time.

# Chapter 2

During her fifteen years specializing in intellectual property law with Kellerman, Keyes, Cohen, Beckers and Flagstone, a leading firm located on Lexington Avenue in New York City, Linn Beckers had risen from a staff attorney to senior partner, affording her a comfortable lifestyle. Laurence Kellerman, the firm's founder and CEO, had taken an early interest in Linn's career development, seeing how deftly she managed her initial negotiations for three of his top clients regarding their copyright infringement lawsuits. Thereafter, her assignments increased dramatically, Linn becoming the go-to attorney for the most severely contentious copyright and patent litigations.

Today, in her corner office, Linn Beckers glanced at a photograph of her father taken last Christmas, thinking about his retirement and impending visit. A host of ideas were running through her mind when her intercom buzzed.

"Brian and Adam are here for your eleven o'clock meeting," her legal assistant announced.

Five minutes later Linn and her associates Brian McKelvey and Adam Jacobson were seated around the conference table in her office, plotting their strategy for the most urgent case on the current agenda.

"Brian, let's review your summary of the Skylar proposal," Linn began.

The young attorney presented his findings from the case research, and his recommended course of action for the negotiations moving forward. Linn hesitated for a moment before responding.

"Fine, Brian, but you haven't included any relevant data about Skylar's previous merger effort with Consolidated Industries, a similar move they attempted several years back. Did I miss something, or …?"

Brian blushed. His body stiffened as he realized the seriousness of omitting the crucial review.

"Sorry, Linn, I don't' know how I overlooked that connection. I'll get right on it."

"Brian, that's a key reference to this entire case," Linn said, adjusting her eyeglasses. "It's vital to our presentation. You've got to check these connections more thoroughly." She stood up. "Please get on it so we can finish this discussion before the end of the day."

Brian nodded, and he and Adam rose to leave. Brian had started his career with the firm only a year earlier. Although this incident was not his first oversight, Linn believed he was a promising young attorney worthy of her patience and coaching. Her European-style sophistication and intrepid attention to even the most arcane elements of cases never diminished her concern about the development of the associates on her team. On the way back to their offices, Brian and Adam grabbed coffee in the break room. "I don't know how she keeps her cool," Brian said. "I mean, you'd think that my missing a crucial angle like that would send her through the goddamned ceiling."

"Hey, dude, I'm not one bit surprised. She bailed out my ass, too, when I started here. And I think I've mentioned it before, but when my ex-wife put me through the ringer during our divorce, Linn had my back while I went through therapy and all."

"That kind of support is why she's where she is—our lead attorney," Adam replied.

"Yeah, and old Kellerman's been pretty damned great himself," Brian said. "Laurence's fierce loyalty and guidance jump-started my career."

"Mine too. He's one hell of a guy. He takes a real interest in what we're going through— kind of like a … father," Adam said. "And there's a reason he's received that Law Journal Award *twice*. He's the best there is!"

Brian glanced behind them. "Hey, what about Linn, though?" he whispered. "I don't think she's ever had any personal relationships in her fifteen years with the firm. She's got a killer body, and that cool condominium on Columbus Circle really rocks. But she lives there all alone. I feel sorry for her in a way."

"Kind of sad," Adam said. "I remember that condo from the holiday party she threw a few years back—a real classy place with a view of Central Park. But I think she's so damned focused on her work and career that she's never given herself time to get serious with anyone."

"I agree," said Brian, as they separated at the end of the hallway. "But, damn, I'm glad she is where she is!"

Following a quick lunch break at the deli across Lexington Avenue, Linn was back in her office, reviewing the calendar on her desktop. *Just four more days. With mom gone, dad's only interest has been his devotion to his job. What's he going to do now?*

Shortly after joining the firm, Linn became a frequent dinner guest at Laurence Kellerman's home, along with another senior partner, Arthur Keyes, whom she had dated before he became the managing partner. Arthur's high-strung personality and quick temper eventually became turn-offs for Linn, and she broke off their relationship after six months.

In contrast, her fondness for Laurence had grown during her years with the firm. He was a father in absentia. When Linn's mother died, Laurence's concern and empathy comforted her as she worried about her father having to live alone in Brussels at his advanced age. Leopold had met Laurence on two of his visits to New York. Mutually fond of poker, bourbon, and war stories about their respective careers, they became instant friends.

Brushing back her pixie-style, shaggy blond hair, Linn pressed her black-rimmed glasses against her face and scanned the calendar, reviewing the week that lay ahead for her whirlwind tour of the city: Broadway shows, The Mostly Mozart Festival at Lincoln Center, Sardi's, the Met, the Four Seasons, and (her dad's favorite place of all) the Café Carlyle. *I can't wait to be with him and hear about his retirement plans. He's going to be*—

Her desk phone was buzzing.

"Hello."

"Linn, thank God you're here!" Arthur Keyes was frantic. "Come to my office right away!"

Two other senior partners, Kevin Cohen and Randall Flagstone, were there when she arrived. Arthur gestured toward the chairs in front of his desk.

"Please."

He closed the door and joined them, loosening his tie as he sat down.

"Laurence Kellerman is missing!"

"*Missing?* How?" Kevin asked.

"He was supposed to be on the 11:20 flight from Vienna this morning. The airline's passenger services representative confirmed they had collected his ticket and issued him a boarding pass. Our driver waited at the gate at Kennedy this afternoon, but Laurence never got off the goddamned plane."

"Look, Art," Kevin replied, "you know he's been forgetting about meetings during the past couple of months and—"

"Right. He even failed to show up in court for that big Minelli case last month," Randall added. "The old guy is over eighty, and yes, he's been slipping lately. I've been concerned about him for weeks now."

"Did they confirm that he actually boarded?" Linn asked. "I mean, if they collected his boarding pass, he must have been identified before boarding."

"I called the airline directly, Linn," Arthur replied. "After half an hour of call transfers and interrogations before accepting my claim as his power-of-attorney, they finally confirmed that he did, in fact, get on the flight. And they told me that no one got off the plane before it took off. How the hell could this possibly happen?"

"The only think that comes to mind, Art, is … a look-alike," Linn suggested.

7

Kevin and Randall laughed at Linn's proposed intrigue. Arthur's head jerked toward them and back to Linn. His lined forehead twitched as he spoke, his face awkwardly close to hers.

"Why in God's name would that ever happen? What the hell kind of scenario are you thinking of, Linn?"

"Slow down a bit, Art, and look at the facts. The agent collected Laurence's ticket, and he presented his boarding pass at the gate. No one left the plane before take-off. Isn't this a logical path to follow right now? Couldn't someone *disguised as Laurence* have gotten on the plane, and then—in the restroom just before exiting the plane—changed back to his *own appearance*? Am I missing something? Or did Laurence parachute out of the goddamned 737!"

"Linn, I … I'm sorry. I didn't mean to—"

"Forget it, Art. Let's just calm down and think about what to do next."

"You may be on to something, Linn. Detective Cummings helped us with a few of our cases over the years, and they included some off-the-wall stuff—even a kidnapping. He's the guy we need right now to get a handle on this insanity. In the meantime, Kevin, how about you hustling down to travel and getting Laurence's itinerary for his Vienna trip—the hotel, side trips, restaurant reservations—the whole nine yards."

"I'm on it, Art."

"Let's get together in about an hour and go over everything. Linn, could you just give me a minute? See you guys later."

"Sure, Art."

"Damned good call, Linn. Thanks."

"You know I've got a suspicious nature, boss. And remember, my dad's a detective. It's in my blood." He watched Linn as she turned and strode toward the door—her firm, slim hips swaying, her shaggy hair tossing in the air. *Damn, I miss our times together.*

She turned unexpectedly, catching him gawking.

"I forgot to mention that Dad's going to be in town next week." She was smiling. "Would you like to join us for drinks sometime?"

Arthur smiled back. "Sounds, great! How is the old guy doing? Finally retired, huh?"

"Yep, he did it. Forty-five years with the Brussels Police Department. Can you believe?"

Their eyes met briefly. She winked. "See you in a bit."

"Thanks, Linn." Arthur resumed his gaze as she left.

An hour later the team spread out copies of all of Laurence's travel documents on the twelve-foot-long mahogany conference table, Arthur itemizing them aloud: "reservations for the Hotel Imperial, concert at the Musikverein, lunch at the Belvedere Museum, Café Scharzenberg, dinner at the Palmenhaus, a private jet to Salzburg. Hold on a second—Why the hell's he going to Salzburg?"

"You know how he worships Mozart," Randall responded. "He's probably there on a whim to visit the old Geburtshaus again. Mozart's birthplace is like a shrine to him."

"Right, and he's been one of the major sponsors of the Mostly Mozart Festival since its inception," Linn added. "He rarely misses a concert or lecture at Lincoln Center during the entire month."

Arthur was focusing on the plane reservation as if waiting for a secret code to appear from the *Fly the Friendly Skies* logo atop the page. Kevin broke the silence. "We can contact the folks at Lufthansa and the private jet company to review the flight manifests. Maybe something odd will pop up."

"Let's do it!" Arthur said, snapping out of his trance. "We'll check it all out."

Linn picked up the hotel reservation. "I'll review his stay at the Imperial to see if anything looks out of the ordinary there."

"Great, Linn," Arthur responded. "I am going to Laurence's place to check on things there. Oh, and Linn, get his office phone logs from the past month, too. We'll put our heads together again around four o'clock—three hours should be enough time to find out where we are on all this crap. I've called Mike Cummings at the precinct and asked him to join us. He's been a huge help to us for years whenever our clients' witnesses went missing. He's a great guy, and I know he'll help us out on this one. He and Laurence have been buddies for decades."

9

# Chapter 3

Later that afternoon, Arthur Keyes and his team gathered in the conference room with Detective Michael Cummings, trying to piece together the puzzle laid out before them.

"Thanks for coming on such short notice, detective," Arthur began.

"Hey, you know how much I love the old guy. Whatever I can do—I'm here to help."

"Okay, folks, let's see where we are with all this," Arthur resumed. "I combed through Laurence's condominium—neat as a pin, of course, like always. The old man's been living alone in that apartment since Gayle died eleven years ago, and I swear the housekeeper must clean the place every day! Everything seems to be in perfect order: no notes on his desk, nothing unusual in his den, nothing out of place. But his library is enormous; it would take us a month to go through all those bookcases and cabinets. I'll have to go back there again." He turned to Linn. "Anything suspicious in his phone logs or hotel stay?"

Linn propped her elbows on the table. "It seems a bit odd that Laurence didn't spend much time in Vienna at all. I spoke with the hotel manager, and damn, after spending fifteen minutes proving who I am and documenting my position in this firm, he finally consented to supply at least a bit of information. He said that Laurence hadn't picked up his room key for three days. And the housekeeping staff reported that he never seemed to have occupied his room after the first night: towels still in place, bathroom spot clean, bed not drawn down—nothing!"

"Kevin, what about the air travel?"

"Well, Linn's report kind of stacks up with what I've found. It looks like Laurence took a private jet to Salzburg on Friday, the day after he arrived in Vienna. The jet company's manifests show that he didn't go back to Vienna until the following Monday, the day before he was scheduled to return home to New York."

"You see, folks, the missing link here is the ground transportation in Salzburg," said Detective Cummings, who had been examining the schedules and reservations. "What happened when he got off that private jet from Vienna? The trail runs cold right there!" A savvy veteran of thirty years with the NYPD, Cummings had managed every kind of case imaginable during his career, from celebrity kidnappings to terrorist bombings. Laurence was a longtime supporter and a frequent donor to the Police Benevolent Association, and for many years his firm had represented scores of cases involving the NYPD, all pro bono.

"This sounds so weird—not like the Laurence I know at all," Arthur said.

Cummings sorted through the hotel reservations, stopping at the Hotel Imperial, flicking the page in front of him to the top of the pile. "Yes, the missing piece to this entire cluster fuck—uh, sorry Linn—is definitely Salzburg!"

"Detective, no need to apologize for your colorful prose to one who's so well versed," Linn retorted, her response drawing nervous laughter from the others.

"No hotel reservation in Salzburg," Cummings continued, unabashed. "Linn, you said the Hotel Imperial responded that he had not stayed there after the first night, on any of the following three nights. So, the trail hits a dead end at the moment Laurence landed at the Salzburg airport."

Arthur reached over and grabbed the hotel reservation. "How the hell did all of us geniuses miss that clue?"

"That's why they pay me the big bucks, old buddy," Cummings joked.

"Assuming he remained in Salzburg, where the hell would he have stayed?" Linn asked.

"There's where our search must begin," the detective counseled. "We've got to track down everything he did after he got off that jet in Salzburg—everything from shuttles, taxis, limos, and every possible hotel option."

"How the hell is that even possible, Mike?" Arthur asked.

"The impossible is what makes this goddamned job so much fun. I've still got a few contacts at Interpol from the old 9/11 days. Get me copies of all this stuff and I'll start working on it right away. The subway murders can wait!"

Art walked Cummings to the elevator.

"I can't thank you enough for helping us out, Mike. I just can't imagine what the hell is going on with him."

"Listen, Art, no one cares about Laurence more than me. I'll do everything I possibly can to expedite this matter."

When he got back to the conference room, Arthur said, "You know, gang, I don't know how the hell that guy keeps so calm and focused. It is absolutely amazing. So, for now, let's all get back to our clients, okay?"

Arthur called Linn back as they were all leaving. "You mentioned cocktails next week. How's Thursday?"

"Sounds fine, Art. Dad will be happy to see you again. We'll pick the place."

# Chapter 4

*About to descend from the landing, Jeff Lambert was shocked by the sight of his brother-in-law standing at the bottom of the stairway. "What the hell are you doing here? Don't point that gun at me, God damn it! Are you out of your fucking mind?"*

*Larry Ingles was about to pull the trigger. "You murdered my sister, and now I'm going to execute you!" he screamed.*

*"No! Stop! You got it all wrong!"*

As so often before, Jeff's wife tried to calm him down. "Honey, you're okay. It's only a nightmare."

But Jeff was already stumbling across the floor into the bathroom. Fumbling with the light switch, he clicked on the light, the image gazing back at him from the mirror reflecting his terror and confusion. Pressing his hand against his chest, he felt for the wound. *I'm losing my mind.*

Margie sat on the edge of the bed, holding her head in her hands. Twenty-four years earlier, after their marriage, Jeff had told her the complete story about the macabre tragedy that occurred on his trip to Brussels. The gory sight of Larry Ingles' head blown apart by his self-inflicted gunshot—brain parts scattered on the floor of the iconic Atomium building—had never escaped Jeff's mind.

Being a psychiatric nurse, Margie was keenly aware of the toll that such long-term stress creates. She had begged Jeff to enroll in the trauma clinic at the university hospital where she had been employed for half of her 30-year career. But Jeff always shrugged it off:

"I'm fine. I've been dealing with this crap for years. Don't worry, honey."

A huge financial inheritance, plus a penthouse condominium, from Margie's brother, Heinrich Winterbottom, a successful international stockbroker based in London until his accidental death two decades earlier, had assured her and Jeff a comfortable and secure lifestyle. But she continued her nursing career because of her love for the profession. Jeff, a certified physical therapist specializing in sports medicine, opened a health club.

Jeff had become increasingly withdrawn over the years, isolating himself from his friends. He was an only child, and both his parents were deceased. Impatient and easily provoked to anger, Jeff alienated clients, causing his business to suffer. Margie often tried to coax him back to playing golf with his old classmates, hoping he'd find it a way to relax. "I can't be bothered with all that meaningless crap," was all he ever replied. Besides Margie, only their son, Christopher, brought real meaning and joy to Jeff's life. Unlike his father, Christopher was not the athletic type, but he did enjoy bowling and going to Phillies or Eagles games on weekends with his dad. And that was all the comfort Jeff needed.

It was in their spacious condominium on Rittenhouse Square, an improbable oasis in the gritty city of Brotherly Love, that Christopher grew up. As a child, he loved playing in his uncle's den, which had remained untouched since Heinrich's death. A lifelong enthusiast of Wolfgang Amadeus Mozart's music, Heinrich had amassed a collection of Mozart recordings, biographies, and souvenir programs from concerts he had attended all over the world. While Margie more than once expressed reluctance to keep Heinrich's vintage Steinway after she and Jeff moved into the condominium, Jeff was adamant about keeping it. "Somehow it feels like Ricky's still here," he'd insist, using the nickname he made up for his brother-in-law. While Heinrich had always protested his use of that nickname, he gradually came to cherish it as a token of Jeff's affection.

By the time he was six years old, Christopher had already spent hundreds of hours listening to Mozart concertos and symphonies on Heinrich's old Magnavox turntable. Even earlier, at age three, he had begun climbing up onto the piano bench, fingering the ebony and ivory keys of his uncle's grand piano.

By age eight, Christopher had learned the basic scales and chords; that same year, he astounded Jeff when he played "Happy Birthday" to him on his 50th birthday. Christopher's piano instructor, a retired pianist from the Philadelphia Orchestra, noted early-on that she was certain the boy had a rare talent. She continued coaching him throughout his early education and was instrumental in developing the skills that led to Christopher's acceptance, at the age of eighteen, to the prestigious Curtis Institute of Music.

During the two years following graduation from Curtis, Christopher performed at recitals and concert venues throughout the Philadelphia metropolitan area. Now, as his 24th birthday approached, he was preparing for a recital in Lincoln Center in New York City at the renowned Mostly Mozart Festival.

By then, Christopher had been dating Julie Chen, a gifted violinist and classmate, for more than a year. Their relationship had grown most serious just at the time Julie's father, David Chen, a top neurosurgeon at the Hospital of the University of Pennsylvania, accepted a position as head of a neuro-research institute in San Francisco. Julie's relocation to the West Coast with her family just two weeks before Christopher's recital in New York blunted his excitement about his debut.

"Mom, I'm really going to miss her. There's something special between us," Christopher told Margie at breakfast on the day he learned of Julie's impeding departure.

"She didn't have a choice in the matter, CJ. She's not yet employed, so remaining in the city would have been quite difficult, especially as she pursues her career. How did you leave it? I mean, what is she saying about your relationship now?"

"Well, we're going to keep in touch. I am certainly not giving up on her. I'm already missing her."

"That's important, honey. She still cares for you. You're both young, and there are so many possibilities for the future. Don't give up, CJ. Things might still work out for both of you. Just stay connected."

"You know I will."

Margie hugged him. "And don't forget to call Matt and Leo about the schedule for New York."

Christopher laughed. "Yeah, right! I'd better call them. Thanks, again, mom."

# Chapter 5

Leo Weber had just stepped out of the shower and was drying himself off when the phone rang. Wrapping the towel around his waist, he trotted down the hall to the bedroom and grabbed the phone on its fifth ring.

It was Christopher.

"CJ! How the hell are ya, kid?"

"Terrific, Uncle Leo. I just wanted to check in with you about the arrangements for my recital at Lincoln Center next week."

"Yeah! Matt and I can hardly wait—Christopher Jeffrey Lambert at the Mostly Mozart Festival! We've booked three rooms for two nights at the old Empire Hotel for all of us. And we're taking you and your parents to Café Fiorello to celebrate afterwards, okay? We could meet you at the hotel on Tuesday. That way you can relax the night before—and the night after—your performance. Are you good with that?"

"Yeah, great. I need to rehearse at Avery Fisher Hall on Wednesday afternoon, so that will work out perfectly. You're the best."

"What would old Mr. Mozart do, right?"

Christopher and Leo were still jabbering when Matt appeared in the doorway. Mid-morning sunlight shining through the window spotlighted Leo's wet, disheveled greyish-brown hair and slim, suntanned back.

"What the hell's going on?" Matt moved closer to Leo, pressing against his towel-draped body.

"I've got the next Lang Lang on the phone. It's about his recital at…"

Matt had tightened his embrace. He rested his chin on Leo's gleaming left shoulder and lifted the phone out of Leo's now limp hand.

"Hey, CJ! How the hell are ya? Ready for your debut on the world stage?"

"As ready as I'll ever be, Uncle Matt. I'm going to be playing the Fantasy—"

"Damned right you are, and like no one's ever freakin' played it before!" A longtime heavy metal and Freddie Mercury fan, Matt, unaware of any difference between "fantasy" and "rhapsody," could relate to only one of them: "rhapsody"—Mercury's Bohemian. "I can't wait to see you up there in those bright lights where you belong, kiddo. And thanks for getting us those primo front row center seats. Leo and I've made all the arrangements. We—"

Leo pulled the phone back, his towel dropping to the floor. "Yeah, he already knows all about it, Matt," Leo whispered. "I just went over everything, uh …"

Matt had started massaging him.

"Are you guys all right?" Christopher asked.

"Sorry … yeah … great, it's all good, CJ. Your Uncle Matt's feeling a bit frisky this morning."

"Well, I'm so looking forward to being with you guys again."

"Us, too. Break a leg, kid!"

"Thanks, guys. See you on—

Matt again commandeered the phone.

"And remember: *practice, practice, practice.*"

Christopher was laughing as Matt hung up the phone.

"Okay, babe, let's, uh … finish toweling off that steamy body," Matt purred.

Avery Fisher Hall's sold-out crowd that included Linn Beckers and her dad buzzed with anticipation at the opening night of the 2014 world-class Mostly Mozart Festival. Christopher was backstage peering out at the audience, soaking in the ambience of the legendary concert hall.

"Good luck, son," the host for the concert said, patting Christopher on the shoulder as she headed onstage to introduce him. Warm applause greeted her arrival.

"Ladies and gentlemen, welcome to the Mostly Mozart Festival. During the past few decades, it has been our distinct pleasure to bring you the greatest celebration in the world of the magnificent composer's work. As part of this venue, it has been our policy to highlight upcoming stars. So, tonight, I am truly pleased to present to you Christopher Jeffrey Lambert, a recent graduate of Philadelphia's Curtis Institute of Music. Mr. Lambert will be performing Mozart's Fantasy in C minor, followed by Piano Sonata Number 14 in C minor."

Christopher strode to center stage, greeted by enthusiastic applause. He looked out at the crowd, and bowed. His heart pounded as he glanced at his teary-eyed mother. Then he turned to the piano, flipping his tuxedo tails behind him as he sat down. He gazed for a moment at the Steinway's gleaming keys, his right arm poised above his head.

*Everything I've ever dreamed of is about to happen right now.*

In an instant his hand fell to the keyboard, striking the first somber note of Mozart's astonishing Fantasy in C minor, seizing the audience's attention. One of the composer's most shocking pieces, the music's radical style foretold—and many musicologists believe, inspired—the brilliance of Beethoven, while maintaining the signature sound and beauty for which Mozart is so renowned. Christopher's fingers moved deftly along the keyboard, the scales rapidly rising and falling, recreating the dissonance and at once harmony that has endeared the genius of Mozart to countless millions for more than two centuries. Gasps emanated from the audience as the Fantasy's haunting melody enveloped the concert hall. The young pianist ended the Fantasy with a flourish, raising both arms high in the air as he rose from the bench. Wild applause greeted the grand finish. Christopher bowed and tapped his hand against his heart. Bowing again, he returned to the piano as the applause continued.

Fixing his eyes on the keyboard, he plunged into the Sonata's first octave. The modulating movements of the adagio clearly showed Christopher's prowess as he navigated smoothly through one of the most complex, embellished melodies imaginable. As he played the opening bars of the tragic final movement, rare in Mozart's compositions, Christopher's own deep feeling of loss at Julie's absence saddened him. He coaxed the brooding sound out of each individual key, eliciting the music's deep emotions from his own heart. His strong right hand led the melody while his smooth, steady, left hand accompanied the musical structure with broken chords, ending the coda in perfect cadence. After remaining motionless for ten seconds, he got up and turned to the audience, which had been raining down bravos from the highest tiers of Avery Fisher Hall.

Jeff, Margie, Matt and Leo rose to their feet, joining the Mozart fans in a standing ovation. Leo turned to Matt. "We just saw our own CJ knock two Mozart fastballs right out of the freakin' ballpark, buddy. These are two seriously tough pieces to perform."

"The kid's a genius!" Matt responded.

The house lights went up as Christopher exited the stage. Jeff took Margie by the hand, Matt and Leo following closely behind as they hurried backstage, where the usher directed them to Christopher's dressing room. Margie tapped on the door.

"Come in," Christopher responded.

When Margie opened the door, Christopher was seated, his eyes closed, his head thrust back against an antique-gold damask armchair framed by two huge arrangements of red carnations and white roses.

"Christopher," Margie sighed as she rushed to him and embraced him. "Honey, we're so proud of you."

"They loved you, CJ," Jeff bubbled, kissing his son on the forehead.

Matt approached with a pen in his hand, brandishing it in the air along with his program.

"May I have your autograph, maestro?"

Christopher shook his head. "You are too much! And thanks for these spectacular flowers." He seized the program with a flourish and inscribed the cover: "To my favorite uncles, Matt and Leo. How could I ever make my debut at Lincoln Center without you? Christopher Jeffrey Lambert." He handed the program back to Matt, but Leo snatched the memento before Matt could react.

"I'll take care of this, buddy. It's much too precious to abandon to your indecipherable filing system.'"

"Yeah, okay. Whatever you say, boss." Matt's cellphone was buzzing. "Hey, it's time for us to leave for our dinner reservations across the street. You must be starving, kid."

"You've got that right. I could eat a horse!"

"I know it's an Italian restaurant, CJ, but I'm not sure Fiorello's features 'horse head' on its storied menu," Matt intoned, in his best impersonation of Brando's Don Corleone.

All howled as they turned to leave the dressing room.

"Wait, what about those gorgeous flowers?" Christopher asked, turning around.

Matt pinched Christopher's cheek. "Not to worry, maestro. It's all taken care of. They will be in your room when you get back to the hotel."

Within ten minutes they were entering the illustrious New York restaurant. Matt approached the maître d'.

"Ah, good to see you again, sir."

"Massimo, how are they treating you tonight?"

"It's been a wonderful evening, Mr. Stephenson."

Matt and Leo had dined at the restaurant three weeks earlier, when they were in the city to see the play *Wicked*. They had rewarded Massimo generously for his promise to have the "Lang Lang" table reserved for this special night.

"Massimo, I want to introduce you to the star of Lincoln Center this evening—my nephew, Christopher Jeffrey Lambert. And to his parents, Margie and Jeff."

"Well, this is indeed an honor, sir. Thank you for choosing Café Fiorello this evening."

"A real pleasure, Massimo," Christopher responded. "It was Matt and Leo's choice, so I know we are in the best of all places tonight."

*"Mille grazie, signore!"*

The maître d' snapped his fingers, and the head waiter appeared. "Good evening, folks. This way, please."

Café Fiorello was packed with its usual array of concertgoers, celebrities, tourists, and residents of the upscale condominiums towering forty floors above it. Heads turned as the tall, slim, tuxedo-clad young man—a shock of silky black hair partially covering his left eye, was escorted with his family to their table. When the waiter had seated everyone, Matt turned to Christopher.

"You're the toast of the freakin' town tonight, pal. Did you see that young blond chick ogling you when you walked in? I thought she'd fall off her chair. ... Don't worry if you *did* notice, dude. I won't breathe a word to Julie!"

Silence fell over the celebration. Christopher looked at Matt, then at everyone around the table, before responding. "Well, ... I know you haven't heard about it yet, but Julie and her family have moved to San Francisco."

"I'm so sorry, kid. I didn't realize that you and she had split."

Leo spoke up. "Leave it to old Uncle Matt to put his size 10 ½ in his mouth right before eating dinner."

"Hey, CJ, I apologize," Matt said.

"Come on, Uncle Matt, don't worry about it. Julie's dad got a top position out there, so they had to relocate. Things may still work out between us. Anyway, that chick over there was looking at *you*, not me."

"I'm not sure you're right about *that*, kid!"

Everyone at the table burst into boisterous laughter, causing heads to turn. Matt began imitating a cop slowing down traffic. "What are you trying to do?—get us thrown out of yet another fine restaurant in New York?"

The waiter took their drink orders. Two minutes later, Jeff was on his feet, raising his glass. Looking across the table at Christopher, he toasted, in a mellow tone, "To you, Christopher, my amazing son, and to the magnificent career that lies ahead for you. We love you!"

"Here, here!" Leo added.

Margie fixed her eyes on Christopher. "You know, honey, I was just thinking about your first encounter with the piano. It wasn't a very auspicious one. You were about four years old when you climbed up onto the piano bench and tried to reach the keyboard of Uncle Heinrich's Steinway. But your arms couldn't stretch that far. You fell, banging your head against the parquet floor. I'll never forget how you screamed! Your uncle purchased that white monstrosity shortly after buying the condominium. And he didn't even know how to play the piano! I begged your dad a dozen times to get rid of it, but he refused."

Jeff patted her wrist. "Yeah, dear, but just think—where would CJ be today without it, huh?"

"Even though I never met Uncle Ricky, it seems I somehow know him," Christopher said.

"That's certainly understandable," Margie replied, "since I had to drag you out of his den more often than I can remember. You were always getting into his stuff—pulling out of his desk and closets old programs and memorabilia from those Mozart concerts he attended all around the world."

Jeff stopped sipping his gin and tonic. "And let's be honest, Margie. CJ was intrigued by that 'white monstrosity' from the first time he set his eyes on it. The morning after he fell off the bench, in fact, he was in the living room exploring the scene where he had left off. You heard him banging on the keys with both hands, and, startled as the notes sounded, he screamed for you to come into the living room."

"Ricky was one in a million," Matt mused. "He was always so damned generous. It was fantastic that you inherited his spectacular condominium and all, but, to this day, I cannot understand how he ever pulled off that humongous deal to save Riley's House. Leo and I had everything set up to open that drug rehab center for veterans when the bottom fell out at the last minute, and Heinrich rode in to save the day. How the hell he ever found the twenty-one million bucks to do it, I'll never know!"

"Our menu for this evening, folks," the waiter interrupted, handing a bill of fare to each of them. "Please let me know if I can be of any help with your selections."

Leo studied the menu. "This is without a doubt the hottest restaurant in the city," he mused. "They concoct the best damned special appetizers—all displayed up front for our inspection. Just go up there, check them out and point to the delicacies you like most, and they'll appear at our table seconds after we return. You can order entrees from the menu for your main courses."

Jeff stared at Leo. "Man, you guys must own stock in this place!"

"If only!" Matt grunted.

Minutes later, as they all enjoyed the calamari, fresh sardines, clams, roasted red peppers, eggplant and shrimp, Christopher turned to Matt and Leo. "Come on now, guys, this has all been about me tonight. What have you two dudes been up to lately?"

Silence. Leo poked Matt. "*You* tell them."

Matt finished a succulent shrimp, then patted his lips with his napkin. "Well, you all know how much we love the old Green Rock Resort."

"Hell, yeah," Jeff said. "That's where we met—about a hundred years ago!"

Matt reprised his traffic-cop role. "Okay, calm down, Jeff. It hasn't been around quite that long. Leo and I've been running the grand old place for nearly *half* a century now. Can you believe it? But, hey, in two years we'll be freakin' septuagenarians!"

"That's not possible," Jeff exclaimed. "Don't tell me you're gonna—"

The traffic cop signaled again.

"Just take a sip of your G & T, buddy, okay? And let me finish." Matt's voice softened.

"Somebody has just made us an offer we can't refuse. No... no horse's head involved, if that's what you're thinking. With the casino industry expanding, and our resort less than an hour from the city, it's been a prime real estate target for years."

24

Leo cut in. "We've always been fastidious with maintaining and upgrading the place, and it continues to be written up in the travel rags. So, finally, it all makes sense."

"I love that old resort," Margie said. "Do you really mean that you're ready to part with it? That must be a brutally tough decision for you fellas."

"Yo, people, *all things must pass.* Isn't that what George Harrison used to say—before he passed? Anyway, folks, it is time. Leo and I want to see our last sunset on Waikiki Beach! We love our place there but don't get to spend enough time enjoying it."

"Wow! I'm sorry I ever asked *that* question," Christopher said.

Laughter ensued as waiters presented the entrees.

"This saltimbocca is the best I've ever tasted," Jeff said as he savored the first succulent piece of his perfectly cooked veal.

Margie and Christopher enjoyed the Veal Marsala, rating it superb. Leo and Matt beamed, seeing their guests so pleased. Matt ordered another bottle of Barolo.

Jeff turned to Leo. "You know, you fellas hired me to run the health club at Green Rock way back about three decades ago. I had just got my master's in physical therapy and was looking for the perfect job to start my career. And did I ever find it! That's where I met Ricky. You remember me telling you, Margie, I'm sure. Your dad was quite ill at the time, and Ricky was about to take him to Brussels to enroll him in a new clinical trial." Jeff's tone grew somber. "He was searching for a private therapist to take care of him—and there I was! It's still hard to believe how all that happened."

"Yeah, old Heinrich stole you away from us and whisked you off to Brussels," Matt responded. "But it all worked out for the best—for all of us, right?"

"For everyone but Ricky. Poor guy, I still miss him so much," Jeff replied.

Margie held Jeff's arm and kissed his cheek. "But all of that rigmarole brought us together. We have so much to thank Ricky for."

"There'll never be another one like him," Matt said. "Well, the deal we're making gives us our own damned apartment in Green

Rock—for life. So, when we come back to visit, we will always have our place, and we can still gather there and enjoy it."

"Septuagenarians?" Christopher said more loudly than he intended, the wine taking its toll. An elderly couple at a nearby table looked at him.

"The Barolo's gotten to all of us, I'm afraid," Leo said.

"Seriously," Christopher continued, his voice lowered, "you two have more energy than guys I know half your age. And you also *look* so damned young! I mean, you're both trim and athletic. Matt, with your shock of silver, platinum-blond hair, you look exactly like Jon Bon Jovi!"

Matt began singing "Living on a Prayer," the New Jersey singer's popular hit, amid laughter around the table.

"And check out Leo, here," Christopher continued, "With your short brown, grey-speckled mane, and trim physique, you're a dead ringer for Tom Brady!"

Leo arched his arm as if to throw a deep pass to the maître'd.

"But nobody's ever sacked *this* guy," Matt said, elbowing Leo.

"No, but *you've* sure sacked me more than a few times, old buddy," Leo joked.

"And didn't you two dudes co-chair the county's annual fund for homeless veterans last year, raising more than a million bucks?" Christopher went on.

Matt raised his glass of ruby-red Barolo high in the air. "Well, Mr. Lang Lang, you are just too damned kind," he said, "but you can't stop time, no matter how hard you try. It just keeps biting you in the ass. This is the optimum move for us at this pivotal point of our time on earth."

Jeff raised his glass. "To new beginnings!"

"And we're going to get all of you over to the paradise in the Pacific soon. And, Christopher, we'll get you a nice gig there, too!"

"Aloha!" Christopher cheered, the wine finally overtaking him.

"Aloha!" rang out from the table.

As the waiter approached with the dessert menu, Matt waved him off.

"Stefano, no need for the menu. Listen, everybody. These guys make the best Zabaglione in New York City—or even in Florence, for that matter. Let's all have some of that magical concoction, okay?"

"Matt, I can't put another ounce of food in me," said Margie. "I'm stuffed!"

"You won't believe how smoothly that heavenly delicacy will ooze down your throat and find the last bit of open space. You've got to try it."

"Well, okay, if you insist."

"And Stefano, please bring us a bottle of your best Lacrima Christi," Matt added.

"Very good, sir."

After enjoying their luscious dessert, savoring it with the sweet vintage, the now-subdued group fell into a satiated silence.

"Well, it's a damned good thing you booked our rooms across the street," said Jeff, a moment or two later, "because there's no way in hell I could navigate any farther after this magnificent dinner."

Christopher was flying high. *"Abbondanza! Magnifico!* Thanks for one hell of a fantastic evening."

Matt got up, walked around the table, and stood behind Christopher, massaging the young virtuoso's shoulders. "Do you have any freakin' idea how proud and privileged we are to be part of this elite circle tonight, CJ? I mean, here you are having just embarked on a magnificent career, wowing the most sophisticated Mozart crowd in the world, and *we* are in the middle of it all."

"And, my God— at the world class Mostly Mozart Festival!" Leo added.

The restaurant was nearly empty as they made their way toward the front door.

"May I get a taxi for you, Mr. Stephenson?"

"Thanks, Massimo, but we're just across the street."

"Very good, sir. *Buono notte,* everybody. *Grazie!*"

Matthew pressed a Benjamin into Massimo's palm. *"Era squisito, Massimo! Grazie!"*

*"Grazie mille, signore! Arrivederci."*

※

As Christopher entered his hotel room, the lights rising from the massive Lincoln Center, twenty floors below, cast a glow into the room. He flicked the light switch and beheld two brilliant arrangements of red carnations and white roses flanking the sofa.

*Red—Mozart's favorite color! Those guys are just so incredibly thoughtful. And the "Lang Lang" table!*

He walked across the room and leaned on the windowsill. Looking down directly at the soaring fountain in front of the iconic complex of buildings, he let out a sigh. *I never dreamed a night like this could ever happen to me.*

Christopher untied his bow tie and loosened his collar, his gaze still taking in the white marble buildings below. He turned and walked to the dresser. Glancing in the mirror, he looked into his eyes and blinked. *This was all for you tonight, Uncle Ricky.*

Christopher reached into the righthand pocket of his trousers and pulled out a brown leather pouch. He placed it on top of the dresser, extracting from it a pewter cigarette case. With his index finger, he traced the dent at the center of the case as he had done countless times before. He pressed the sides, and it popped open— nothing inside. He handled the mysterious mementos countless times since first discovering them, at age six, in his uncle's storage cabinet. *Uncle Ricky, what odd story could be involved with these keepsakes of yours?* he wondered—the same question that had run through his mind so many times, for although Ricky was known to have been a heavy drinker, Margie said more than once that he had never smoked cigarettes or cigars in his life. In the years since its discovery, the puzzling pewter cigarette case had become a lucky charm for him. Whenever he faced a difficult exam or had to appear in solo performances at school, he would slip the leather pouch containing the pewter case—a kind of heirloom rabbit's foot—into his pants pocket, just as he had done tonight. He placed the cigarette case back into the pouch, then tucked it securely inside his luggage … just as his cellphone buzzed. It was 1:30 in the morning.

"Chris, I know it's late, but I've been thinking about you all night and just wanted to hear how your performance went."

"Julie, are you kidding? It's so great to hear your voice. You've been on my mind all night—even during the recital. I'm … uh … kind of flying right now. My two adopted uncles feted me and my parents to a splendid dinner, and I think I drank more alcohol than I normally drink in a month."

Julie was amused hearing Christopher's slurred response. "Chris, you sound so sexy. I am happy and proud for you. I knew you would dazzle that tough New York crowd."

"Babe, I miss you. God, I wish you were here with me right now."

"Well, one of these nights, soon, we're going to catch up," she whispered. "I know it's late, but I just had to call."

"Any hour, any day, any moment, Julie! I love you, babe!"

"Keep in touch, Chris."

"You know I will, babe. Good night."

Christopher, only partially undressed, dropped into bed, exhausted and intoxicated—less by the Barolo than by the exuberance of the Mostly Mozart crowd. Drifting off to sleep, he was back in the concert hall playing the last four bars of the Mozart Sonata. Then he was rising, turning to face the audience, only to be stunned at the rows and rows of empty seats until—from the farthest spot in the highest balcony—he heard her voice. *I love you, Chris!*

# Chapter 6

Leopold Beckers tossed and turned all night, thinking about the Mostly Mozart concert and, more notably, the young pianist who had performed there. *What kind of unimaginable coincidence is this?* Earlier that day he had begun reviewing the case file on the bloody Atomium tragedy before leaving for New York, and the name "Lambert" remained stuck in his mind. Reading the concert's program, he was struck by the biographical notes on the pianist, so much so that he had lurched forward in his seat. He focused not only on the name itself— Christopher Jeffrey Lambert—but on its unforgettable initials, mouthing them in disbelief: *CJL*, the same letters adorning the pearl-handled knife found at the Atomium twenty-five years earlier.

"Are you okay?" Linn had asked, concerned by his sudden lurch forward.

Beckers assured his daughter that all was well.

At breakfast the next morning, Beckers brooded about the previous night's incident as he enjoyed the spinach and mushroom omelet Linn had prepared. He took a bite of the sourdough toast and sipped the dark-brewed Lavazza coffee.

"What is it dad? You've been unusually quiet this morning. Is everything okay?"

"You're gonna make some guy incredibly happy one of these days, honey. This omelet is spectacular. And you sure do know how to brew a pot of Lavazza to perfection." He diverted his eyes to the table.

Linn was having none of it.

"Don't try pulling that old switcheroo on me, dad. Something's bugging you. I know you well enough to sense it. Come on, you can—"

"Ah! Just like your mother, I could never pull the wool over her eyes either," Beckers interrupted.

"Okay, detective, so—what is it?"

He struggled through the last remaining reluctance to share with her his decades-long odyssey.

"Well, all right. I don't want you to think I'm losing it or anything, but there's a case that's been bugging me for twenty-five years. I just can't let the damned thing go."

Leopold went on to describe the brutal suicide at the Atomium and the trail of blood—the complete gory tragedy that had rattled Brussels at the time.

Linn listened intently, grimacing occasionally at the story's grisly details, until he finished.

"I can certainly understand your preoccupation with it, dad, but how did it all resurface this morning? We just attended a spectacular performance at the Mozart festival, had a lovely dinner at Le Bernardin—now this."

The old detective snapped his fingers. "Well, *that's just it*, you see. The name of the incredible young man who performed last evening is Christopher Jeffrey Lambert. I'm sure that name is associated with the horrid case at the Atomium, especially those initials on the penknife I just described—*CJL*. I'll have to review the information more thoroughly when I get back home."

"What will you do if there's a connection between the pianist and that horrible carnage in Brussels?"

"I'll have to inform the Department and follow through with it—retired or not! Anyway, don't worry about me. I'm okay. Let's just have one hell of a fun week while I'm here."

Linn gazed at her dad with the same awe she had felt for him as far back as she could remember. She leaned over and kissed his cheek. "Here you are in New York City at a Mostly Mozart concert and you're trying to solve a mystery that unfolded in Brussels twenty-five years ago! You never stop fascinating me with the issues you get involved in. I'm so glad you're here, Dad. I've missed you."

"I've missed you, too, and thanks for being so understanding of this nostalgic old coot. I promise I will not involve you in any more of my weird preoccupations while I'm here. So, what are we doing today?"

Linn glanced at her watch.

"We've got to get down to the Guggenheim. A spectacular Warhol exhibit just opened. Then we'll have lunch at Le Cirque. We have matinee tickets for *Phantom*. Then, you remember Art—from my firm—he's going to join us for cocktails this afternoon at the Top of the Rock."

"Ah, you sure know how to pamper your old man."

※

As the two entered the 6th Avenue side of 30 Rockefeller Center later that afternoon, a voice called out: "Linn!" Arthur Keyes was approaching them, his hand extended to Leopold. "What a terrific delight to see you again, Mr. Beckers. Welcome back to New York!"

"Arthur, how good to have you join us."

Arthur turned to Linn, pecking her on the cheek. "How's your day been?"

"I'll tell you all about it, but we'd better get up to the restaurant and sit down before dad and I collapse."

"Right this way, folks," Arthur said, leading them toward the ornate art deco elevators across the corridor.

When they stepped out on the 65th floor and entered the restaurant, the host escorted them to a cozy table with a view of the Empire State building gleaming sixteen blocks away.

"This is always such a magnificent place to visit," Leopold exclaimed as he admired the skyline. "I remember our first time up here, Linn—with your mother. Remember how thrilled she was—especially by the sight of those magnificent twin towers in the distance? How horrible the way they were so tragically destroyed!"

Arthur erupted, pounding the table with clenched fists. "Those goddamned barbarians tried to destroy this city. I watched those towers collapse, and I still have nightmares about that disaster. That inferno annihilated four of my best friends. God damn those animals that did it!" Linn placed her hand on Arthur's arm. Tears formed in his eyes as he continued. "Sorry, but I'll never get over the hell they wreaked on us that day. It still seems impossible it could have happened." He ran his hands across his face, trying to compose himself. "I don't want to throw a damper on your celebration, but the horror of that day just keeps coming back. I'll never get over it."

"Nor will most of the world, I suppose," Leopold replied. "But for you, being right here in the midst of that disaster—it's so much worse."

"Sorry for that, and thanks for putting up with my obsession. But, look, let's talk about you two. What have you been up to all day?"

"We visited that Marilyn Monroe silk screen exhibit," Linn began. "And Warhol's legendary Campbell Soup cans still dazzle me—sheer genius! After that we took in a matinee of *Phantom of the Opera*. I never, ever tire of hearing that magnificent score. But *this* is the highlight of the day—being up here with my two favorite guys."

Arthur was thrilled to hear those words from Linn. In a moment of light banter, tired from the day's activities, Linn had, for the first time in years, referred to him in personal terms.

"And this is certainly my favorite time of the day," Leopold chimed in, catching a glimpse of their fleeting intimacy. He worried about his daughter being alone as she grew older, and was sorely disappointed when she had told him, four years earlier, that she and Arthur had broken off their brief relationship. "So, do the two of you come up here often?" he asked, addressing Arthur.

"Uh, no, Leopold," Arthur stammered. "But I do love it up here. You know, on 9/11, we were all so damned scared that those suckers were gonna take down this building too."

"For sure, Arthur. The world seemed to be holding its breath on that dreadful day. But tell me, what the hell has old Kellerman been up to these days? Linn told me about that great Minelli contract you snagged a couple of years ago. *Mazel tov!*"

Arthur was squirming, avoiding eye-contact with Leopold.

The waiter, arriving, saved the moment.

"Drinks are on me," Arthur said.

"Then I'll have a French 75," said Linn, ordering the cocktail she enjoyed on her first date with Art.

Leopold ordered a Bourbon and Branch.

"Double that," Arthur said. "Bourbon is exactly what I need right now."

"So, Art," Leopold continued, "you were about to say?"

"Yeah, well, about Kellerman. He's always been a bit strange, as you know. And he's getting up there—81 years old this year. You know, it's always been a 'What the hell is the old man gonna do next?' kind of thing."

"Eighty-one! He's older than me."

"*Way* the hell older," Linn quipped.

Leopold prodded. "Well, Arthur, what's the latest on the old man?"

Arthur had polished off his bourbon in two gulps and was signaling the waiter for a refill. "You're not going to believe the insane situation he's gotten himself into now, Leopold. He goes to Vienna for a brief holiday. Then—"

"Are you, uh, sure you want to get into all of this now, Art?" Linn cautioned. "I mean, aren't we waiting for more information and—"

But Arthur was already pitching forward. "I don't want to burden you with all this, Leopold, but given your professional experience, maybe you could advise us on how to proceed."

"Okay, now you've got me," said Leopold, eager for details. "You can't leave all this up in the air, and we are pretty damned high up already. Let's hear it."

Arthur hoisted his second drink, gulping a good measure of it. "I know you've seen more unbelievable crap than either of us can imagine. But how the hell can *even you* explain something like this?" Leopold studied Arthur's face as the harried attorney spewed out the details of the astounding Salzburg odyssey of Laurence B. Kellerman. After twenty minutes or so, having finished his tale and final ounce of Bourbon, he stopped.

Leopold waited for a moment before responding. "Well, Detective Cummings hit the nail right on the head. The obvious clue to beginning the search is to find out what happened to Laurence when he got off that plane in Salzburg. I've got a couple of friends in Salzburg, both of them old-timers. I can shake a few bushes to see what I can find out. Of course, I would have to coordinate with Cummings on this—it's standard protocol—and together, maybe we can figure something out."

"Leopold, you just took down your damned shingle, ... and here you are jumping headfirst into some outrageous international intrigue." Arthur's words were surprisingly unslurred.

Linn tapped his hand as she addressed her father. "I think we may be a bit *too* high in the sky right now. How about we share a taxi home?"

"Honey, you've always had a way with words," Leopold replied. "You were meant to be a lawyer from the day you were born. I think you entered this world arguing with the obstetrician about the bill your mom received!"

"She's one hell of a gal, Leopold. You sure raised her well."

"Yeah, and she'll be a great catch for some lucky guy one day." Leopold winked.

Once home, Linn asked, "What was all that about—'She'll be a great catch' and all? Have you started a new career as matchmaker?"

"You know, honey, you could do a hell of a lot worse. I mean, Art is a—"

"Now hold it right there, Mr. Cupid, let's not get carried away."

"Well, I'm just saying—"

"Forget it, Dad. I've got a nice quiche Lorraine in the fridge. Let's just stay home and enjoy it."

"Now that's the best idea I've heard all afternoon," he said, settling into the recliner. "I think I've already gained about ten pounds on this trip."

Sitting at the kitchen counter, nibbling on the quiche, complemented by a marvelous White Bordeaux, Linn grew serious. "Dad, I'm worried about Laurence. This is all too mysterious. It seems like he's gotten into something way over his head."

"The solution to every case begins with one good clue, Linn. If we can track him down at his arrival in Salzburg, we may have a shot. I'll see what I can find out. Try not to worry so much about him right now."

"Well, it's not just Laurence. I'm concerned about Art, too. I never talked with you about it, but he became the son that Laurence never had. He and Gayle had no children. After Art's dad was killed in action in Vietnam, Laurence took Art under his wing. It was Laurence who guided him into the legal profession. Although he was an outstanding student all through elementary school, his grades plummeted during his sophomore year in high school after his dad's death. He started taking drugs. Only his mom's love and constant support saved him. She got him the best therapist she could find, and, by the end of the year, Arthur had found a new purpose in life—joining the ROTC, vowing to emulate his dad's bravery in the military."

"Well, that explains his reaction to my 9/11 remarks at lunch. Sorry I raised that topic."

"He's a dyed-in-the-wool native New Yorker, dad. I don't think he'll ever recover. Anyway, Art's father had a tremendous career as an investment broker, providing well for his family; and coupled with his multi-million-dollar life insurance policy, they were financially secure after his death. And, remarkably, Arthur ended up graduating from high school in the top one percent of his class of 1,200 students. He was accepted by all of the Ivy League universities; but because of his love for New York, and wanting to stay close to his mother, he chose Columbia, graduating summa cum laude and passing the bar exam. It was Laurence who guided him into the legal profession."

"What a story! He's even more remarkable than I thought."

"Okay, don't get started on the matchmaker thing again. Well, of course, it was a forgone conclusion that Art would enter Laurence's firm, and soon he became the Kellerman team's go-to attorney. Laurence trusted him with the most confidential matters pressing his firm. As contract attorneys, they represented dozens of famous celebrities and corporate officials. Laurence relied on Art to manage his personal transactions as well. After his wife died, Laurence became increasingly dependent on him."

"Well, I can see why you have such … admiration for him."

"There you go again! How about a slice of that hazelnut torte we bought at Zabar's yesterday afternoon? I'll make some coffee."

"I'm gonna have to go on a diet after this trip. But, sure, bring it on!"

Leopold continued his probing. "There's something there between you two—and you know it. Go with your heart, Linn"

"Okay, okay, but this insane episode has thrown our office off kilter, and I sure as hell hope we can get things resolved soon."

Leopold yawned. "Your old dad isn't used to this kind of pampering. And certainly not the frenetic schedule. I'm afraid I am quite exhausted."

She kissed him on the cheek. "I can't tell you how fantastic it is to be with you, dad."

"Ha! Double that for me. And I even get a missing-person-case to work on in my retirement."

# Chapter 7

First thing in the morning, Leopold phoned his friend Karl Gerber. The intelligence agent had begun his government service in Austria around the same time Leopold started his career in Brussels. They had met at an international law enforcement conference in Vienna two decades earlier.

"*Guten Tag*, Karl. Are you still on the job?"

"Sure am, Leopold. And are you still retired? Wasn't it the day before yesterday?"

"Of course! And already I'm in New York visiting my daughter— just one of the great perks of getting off the old treadmill, Karl. So, what's going on with you over there in Austria?"

Silence.

"Gerber?"

"Well, the government ... just completed its new realignment. All of us locals are now under the total control of the *Bundespolizei*—the country's main federal law enforcement agency."

"Oh, I forgot that was happening."

"Yeah, we're part of the Federal Police of Austria now, and, as you can imagine, it's shaken things up a bit—to say the least."

"What happens to *you* now?"

"Not so bad for me, but things are changing rapidly, and I'm not sure I like the direction we're headed in. It all seems terribly screwed up, you know. So, the way things appear right now, I might be joining you in La La Land sooner than I expected."

"Well, I sure hope everything shapes up for you. It's been a—"

"Oh, I'll be fine. I have been planning to get out of here next year, so—no big deal. In any case, I'm sure you're not calling to ask what the weather's like in the Alps, old friend."

"Just like that tough policeman I've always known. Yes, in fact, there is something I was hoping you can help me with."

Beckers went on to explain the strange situation involving Laurence Kellerman's disappearance. Fifteen minutes later he listened for a response.

"Are you still there, Karl?"

"You just never stop. Do you?"

"I know, I know, but this is a favor for a dear friend. If I could just get a clue on what happened to the old guy when he got off the plane that night in Salzburg, I might be able to start tracking him down."

"*Jawohl!*"

"So, Karl, ... does that mean you can help me out?"

"I'll do everything I can while trying to make a living with the *Bundespolizei*."

"*Danke*, old friend. Keep up the excellent work."

"All for the greater good of the Federal Republic! I'll get back to you after checking out a few things."

"*Danke Schön, Karl. Wiedersehen!*"

"*Bitte schön, mein Freund. Wiedersehen!*"

The next day, Linn booked lunch at Sardi's, as her father requested. It had been his late wife's favorite restaurant ever since their first trip to New York City. Afterward, Linn and Leopold took in a matinee at the Majestic, catching the eternally popular *Les Misérables*. They then joined Arthur for cocktails at the Marriott Marquis, overlooking Times Square.

"We've gotta stop meeting like this," Linn teased.

"It's not like we've done it a thousand times," Art retorted.

"You two should do this more often—without the papa sitting between you."

"Okay, dad, now cut that out. Why don't you tell Art the real reason for our meeting?" She turned toward the window, scanning the vast, flamboyant billboards blazing across the entire city block.

"Listen, Art," Beckers began. "I've spoken with a longtime friend in Salzburg about the situation. If anybody can get a lead on this crazy caper at the airport, he's the guy who can do it. I expect to hear from him before I return to Brussels next week. Anyway, you'll be the first to know."

"Leopold, you're a lifesaver!"

"I'm not a savior *quite yet*, my friend, but I'll do whatever I can to help."

"Cheers to that!" Arthur exclaimed, clinking his bourbon Manhattan a tad too hard against Leopold's.

"Take it easy, Art! You don't want that old blood pressure perking again."

"Not to worry, Linn. Your dad has already helped me calm down more than you know."

# Chapter 8

The following afternoon Arthur returned to Kellerman's home. The echoes of Laurence's loud bantering and infectious laughter were gone, but he could feel his best friend's presence as he scanned the elegant 5th Avenue penthouse. Closing his eyes for a moment, he conjured up Laurence's image—thinking about the last time they met in the apartment before Laurence left for Vienna, listening to Mozart's Jupiter symphony in the den. *Yes! Why the hell didn't I think of that sooner?*

He raced through the living room and down the hallway to the back of the apartment, coming to an abrupt halt at the door of his longtime mentor's den. As so many times in the past, he turned the doorknob gently, as if fearing to disturb Laurence at his desk.

Arthur scanned the room, stopping at the huge mahogany bookcase, its shelves filled with hundreds of legal tomes, their decorated spines the only color in the renowned attorney's otherwise staid man cave. Fastened to the center of the middle shelf was a white marble bust of Wolfgang Amadeus Mozart. Arthur walked directly to the small sculpture and grasped its head, twisting it clockwise, exposing a small black button in the base. He pressed it. The panel of the bookcase behind the sculpture slid open to the left, revealing the 10"-square metal door of a safe built into the wall. He punched in the numbers 6-26-12-5-91 on the safe's keypad. Following a dull whirring sound and beep, the door popped open. His eyes widened as he peered inside. "It's gone!"

※

Laurence Kellerman had been an admirer of Wolfgang Amadeus Mozart's music ever since his senior year at Columbia University, where, for the first time, he attended a classical music concert—featuring the great composer's Jupiter Symphony. His devotion to the study of the composer's life and music became an obsession with him that deepened as he grew older. Kellerman drew strength from the beauty and dramatic tone of the music during the most tragic times in his life. After his parents died, he selected the Mozart Requiem for their public memorial service at St. Patrick's Cathedral, reprising that choice years later for his beloved wife's Mass after her death. The archdiocesan choir, joined by members of the New York Philharmonic, performed the sacred work.

Laurence often spoke with Arthur about the countless evenings he spent alone in his den, comforted by his treasured collection of Mozart recordings. As plans for the creation of the Mostly Mozart Festival unfolded, he became one of the first major sponsors of what, after just a few seasons, became a world-acclaimed annual celebration of Mozart's creations.

Arthur thought about the story Laurence had shared with him twenty-five years earlier about a secret he had learned from one of his closest friends, Oliver Yates, an MI6 agent stationed in London. Someone had found the missing fragment that had been torn off from the bottom right-hand corner of the second-to-last page of the original manuscript of Mozart's Requiem. It had been stolen while on public display during Expo '58, the Brussels World's Fair. Yates told Laurence that the fragment was being shopped around on the underground market; its value was so great, he explained, "because it contains the last four words that Wolfgang Amadeus Mozart ever wrote."

"Oliver Yates is the proud son of a police detective," Laurence had informed Arthur. "And he worshipped his grandfather, who had risen to the rank of Superintendent in the London Police Department." He went on to explain how Yates had served two years in the British Navy before joining the Met Police in London. He rapidly rose through the ranks, becoming the detective in the Criminal Investigation Unit, then, an agent in the MI6 Secret Intelligence Service. "That man," Laurence emphasized, "served loyally for 23 years before suffering severe psychiatric problems following the sudden death of his wife. His best friend, David Corbyn, was a godsend to him, but drugs were Oliver's ultimate source of relief from his inconsolable loneliness. Eventually his dependency drove him to the underground market for his drug supply. DEA agents apprehended him as he tried to buy cocaine on a subway platform in Queens in 1981.

"That's when I met Oliver Yates," Laurence continued. "I was working as a volunteer for the Citizens Support for Law Enforcement legal assistant team when I argued his case before the court, winning a 'not guilty' verdict, which saved his career and reputation. We became close friends during the years following the trial, staying in close contact by phone and, sometimes, on visits to him when traveling in the UK on business or vacation. When Oliver learned from a colleague in Brussels that the missing Mozart fragment was for sale on the black market, he immediately thought of me. He was keenly aware of my longtime fascination with the great composer's music. Hell, I even coerced the big fellow to attend Mozart concerts. So it was Oliver who made it possible for me to obtain Mozart's last words! November 29, 1989 was the most exciting day for me since my wedding day! You're the only person in the world I can trust with the knowledge of this sacred, potentially troublesome mission."

Two weeks later, Arthur—accompanied by retired museum curator Bruce Kasterling, Laurence's longtime friend—met with the seller of the fragment in a conference room in Laurence's Lexington Avenue office.

As he stared into the empty safe, Arthur's thoughts returned to that meeting: how the seller had removed a brown leather pouch from his jacket pocket, withdrawing from it a pewter cigarette case—dented in the center. The seller, Heinrich Winterbottom, set the case on the table, pausing a few seconds before pressing the sides. The case sprung open, revealing the Mozart fragment. Arthur pictured the curator's jaw drop as he gazed at the jagged piece of parchment, studying its color and shape—and words. Kasterling then unzipped a wallet-size black leather case, from which he extracted a pair of tweezers. Ever so carefully, he raised the fragment to the light.

"God in heaven! *There's the watermark!* Beyond any doubt, this fragment is part of Mozart's original autograph manuscript. It was stolen from the Austrian government's exhibit at the Brussels World's Fair in 1958. Experts have noted how cleanly the fragment was removed from the page without affecting anything on it—not any stave, not even a bar-line! Imagine Mozart on his own deathbed feverishly composing a Mass for the Dead for someone else's funeral. As his trembling, swollen fingers slid to the margin of the manuscript, he scribbled the final words he would ever write: 'quam olim d. C:'—the words on this fragment we're looking at right now!"

The curator went on to explain that the phrase "quam olim" is Latin for "which once," the first two words of the fugue "Which once you promised to Abraham and to his seed," the last sentence of the refrain to several of God's promises in the Requiem's Offertory. The letters "d." and "C" are abbreviations for the musical term "da capo," meaning "repeat from the beginning"—in this case, the beginning of the "Quam olim" fugue.

Arthur recalled the curator's solemnly intoned closing remarks: "After he wrote "*quam olim d. C:,*" the quill fell from Mozart's hand. Those were the last words he ever wrote—the very ones on the fragment stolen a century and a half after the great composer's death. And now—*we have them!*"

Dazed by what he had just heard, Arthur turned to Heinrich Winterbottom and asked his permission to take the Mozart treasure to an adjacent room where Laurence, wishing to keep his identity secret, had sequestered himself. Arthur would never forget Laurence's face as he cradled in his hands the pewter cigarette case bearing the precious fragment. Seconds later, Laurence agreed to the price. Arthur presented a bank check for $21 million to Heinrich Winterbottom, completing the transaction.

The curator carefully placed the fragment into a museum-quality, thin acrylic sleeve, resembling a laboratory slide, then returned the leather pouch and pewter cigarette case to Heinrich.

Laurence Kellerman deposited the fragment inside the safe in his den—transforming the steel chamber into a veritable tabernacle. Laurence once confided to Arthur about how he would often retreat to his den, lock the door, and remove his sacred treasure from the safe. He would gaze upon it, meditating as he listened to the beloved composer's Requiem through the world-class Klipsch audio system installed specially for that very ritual, the room transformed into a resounding cathedral.

After Bruce Kasterling's death, in 2011, Arthur Keyes was the only other person who knew the story— and the location—of the Mozart fragment.

"What could the old man possibly be up to now?" Arthur wondered aloud, still staring into the empty space.

He locked the safe, pressed the black button, closing the panel, and rotated the head of the Mozart bust to its original position, tightening it firmly. Then, plopping into Laurence's chair, he swiveled it from side to side, scanning the room in a fruitless attempt to figure out what to do next.

*If I talk to anyone about Laurence's role in this insane Mozart scheme, I risk implicating him in a serious international criminal conspiracy. And yet, it sure looks like the fragment is the reason Laurence went to Vienna—and probably explains his disappearance. He may have been kidnapped, or even—*

Arthur leaped from the chair and out of the room. Seconds later he was in the elevator. *I've got no choice. I must tell Leopold! He's the only one who can tell me what to do next.*

※

"Mr. Keyes!" Cynthia Lamont called out, interrupting her boss's dash toward his office, "you've had an important call from a 'Mr. Beckers' while you were out. He—"

"Beckers! What's the message?"

"Only to call as soon as you can. Here's his cellphone number."

Arthur snapped it out of her hand and bolted into his office, a perfunctory 'Thank you' trailing in his wake.

"Leopold, I just got your message. I was thinking about you and—"

"Ah, the lawyer's ESP talent has always fascinated me!"

"I wish I had even a smidgen of it, my good friend—especially now!"

Leopold hesitated before continuing in his deep, baritone voice. "I have some disconcerting information about Laurence's journey to Salzburg, I need to go over it with you—in person."

"You've heard from your friend in Salzburg already?"

"Art, you know the *Bundespolizei* don't fool around."

"Damn right, Leopold! Well, come over right now."

"Do you want Detective Cummings to join us?"

"No!" Arthur snapped. "I mean, I'd like to speak with you privately. I've got to tell you about a serious matter that *I've* just discovered."

"Now I truly feel like I'm back at my old oak desk in Brussels! I'll be right there, Art."

Leopold grabbed his jacket and walked out to the living room. Linn was slicing a lime.

"Sorry to have to delay cocktail hour, honey. I've got to see Arthur about Laurence's situation. He has urgent news for me—and I've got a news flash for him."

Linn put her hand on his shoulder. "Are you sure you don't want to extend your vacation a bit, dad?"

"Ah, yes, vacation! Who knows what will happen next?" Leopold kissed her on the cheek and headed for the door.

Arthur was alone in the office when Leopold arrived.

"God, I'm glad you could come over, Leopold! I feel bad about getting you involved in all this. I mean, you're supposed to be enjoying you first retirement holiday, and here you are embroiled in international intrigue."

"Now, don't tell Linn, but this is becoming the highlight of my trip—you know—a busman's holiday!"

"Yeah, but you were supposed to have turned in the keys to the 'old bus' last week. And here you are—"

"Let's sit down and review this *mishigas*, Art. I think we may have a severe problem on our hands."

"Okay, excuse me for a moment."

Arthur locked the main entrance to the office and returned. He and Leopold sat across from each other at his conference table.

"Art, I've had some disturbing news from my friend Karl, in Salzburg. He obtained video surveillance footage of the airport from the night Laurence's plane landed. After Laurence deboarded, he was escorted to a black Mercedes by a uniformed driver."

"Well, okay, that's not bad."

"I'm afraid it is. The license was traced to *Ein Volk*, a Neo-Nazi cartel that's been operating in Europe for the past ten years."

"Neo-Nazi?"

"It's a syndicate that's trafficking in stolen art and cultural artifacts. All to finance its political and terrorist agenda. They've got strategic resources within most of the EU and Russia. The cartel's formed an intricate network of professionals—experts in art appraisal— who work hand-in-glove with thieves, most of them retired military personnel, skilled in gaining entrance to the most advanced security systems in the world."

Arthur listened in disbelief. "But how the hell could Laurence have ever gotten involved with a group of thugs like that? He's a brilliant attorney from New York who spends the bulk of his free time enthralled by Mozart's music. It just … it doesn't make any goddamned sense, Leopold."

"He might've had no choice. It seems it was the cartel that decided to get involved with *him*. Laurence may own— or at least know the location of—some valuable piece of art they're looking for. That might be the connection here."

"Well, okay. Now it's *my* turn! This is going to blow *your* mind, Leopold."

"Go on."

"For twenty-four years now, I've kept a secret Laurence entrusted with me. I fear I'm about to betray that trust. But I can't see how I can do anything else, given what a shit show he's now got himself involved in."

Arthur got up, paced around the room, and dropped back down in his chair. Blushing like a young boy about to confess his first mortal sin to the parish priest, he began relating the story of the Mozart fragment. "So, when I opened that goddamned safe today and found it empty," he concluded, twenty minutes later, "it seemed clear then, and what you are saying now confirms it: That's why the old man went to Austria."

"You mean you've actually *seen* the Requiem fragment?"

"Yeah, I was the … *conduit* … between the seller and Laurence."

"You know what, Art? My parents took me to Expo '58. I was a kid in grammar school, so even though I've seen the exhibit, I really have no recollection of what the manuscript looked like. My mother, though … wow, she genuflected in front of the Requiem Mass manuscript like she was facing the grand altar in St. Peter's Basilica! And I'll never forget the turmoil that erupted in Brussels when that Mozart incident hit the newspapers. It was a bombshell— an international uproar! I think it may have been the reason I decided to become a detective. Now you're telling me you've not only *seen* the fragment, but participated in its *theft?*"

"Whoa, now ... wait a second, my friend. *Theft?* Hell no! It was available on the black market. Some Mozart fanatic—no, some *crook!*—tore the fragment right out of the fucking manuscript and sold it to the highest bidder. And who the fuck *knows* where it is now?"

"You've just given a pretty damned good definition of the word 'theft,' my friend," said Leopold, his tone now more serious. "If Laurence loves Mozart so damned much, Art, why the hell didn't he turn the fragment over to the authorities in Austria so it could be returned to its rightful place in history—you know—complete the Requiem manuscript again, once and for all? Then the entire world could enjoy it."

Arthur squirmed and cleared his throat, unnerved at finding himself, despite all his years in the courtroom, suddenly under the pressure of interrogation—with no plausible explanation of his innocence. Not that he didn't try to provide one.

"Come on, now, Leopold. Think about it. How would Laurence ever be able to explain to the government of Austria how he happened to get his hands on the fragment? Seriously, the old man plunked down $21 million so he could worship the damned thing—not to be musicology's Good Samaritan."

"You and your boss have gotten yourselves in one hell of a complicated, and— sorry to say, my friend—extremely dangerous escapade. Just listen to the rest of what I've got to tell you."

"There's more?"

"My friend in Salzburg tracked the surveillance tapes for all traffic in and out of the Salzburg airport during the entire week Laurence was there. Laurence took the departing flight to Vienna *before* he returned to New York."

"Wait ... wait a second, Leopold. I'm quite sure that Laurence *didn't* return to New York!"

"How could you know that?"

Arthur told him how the firm's chauffer—standing as close to the door of the customs checkout as the guard would allow—waited for well past an hour after all the passengers had left and the agents had locked the doors, but Laurence never appeared.

Leopold lowered his head and drummed his fingers on the table. The silence that fell over the room spooked Arthur. "What is it? Why so quiet suddenly?" he asked.

"Well, that's just it, Art. We don't know who arranged the switch, you see. Was it Laurence, perhaps trying to cover his tracks, or … the cartel?"

"The goddamned cartel, they could've—"

"Let's not get ourselves too hacked out about this right now, Art. We've got to think clearly and try to figure out what happened there. Laurence traveled to Austria for a specific purpose. You said you believe that he took the fragment with him. He met with the cartel in Salzburg, returned to Vienna, and on the following day, flew back to New York. Or at least that's what my source says. Yet, no one knows what happened to him. So now—"

"But as I've pointed out, our chauffeur waited more than an hour at the gate," Arthur interrupted. "Laurence never appeared."

"What if someone *posing* as Laurence entered the plane in Vienna—that would explain how he gained entrance to the flight with a bogus copy of Laurence's passport. And before getting off the plane at Kennedy, the impostor was able to alter his appearance. Maybe he went into the restroom, changed his jacket, put on a wig or something—just before deplaning. You know how frantic people become on planes as soon as that tone sounds announcing it's okay to unfasten seatbelts. They jump out of their seats, grab their overhead bags, and push their way to the exit like they're trying to escape a disaster. Who would notice anything? That way, he could walk to the gate unidentified. No CCTV footage would show anyone who looked at all like Laurence. The chauffeur would have been clueless."

Arthur shook his head. "Leopold, that's exactly what Linn suggested when we first learned of Laurence's disappearance last week—and it really knocked me for a loop. I even barked at her for such a weird, off-the-wall idea."

"Ah, yes, the acorn and the tree—I'm damned proud of that brilliant acorn of mine!"

"Man, you detectives! I don't know what the fuck to think now."

"A few things are in play here, Art. First, the Mozart fragment: Where is it? And, of course, where's Laurence? At this point we can't explain his whereabouts from the time he arrived at the Salzburg airport to the day he— if in fact it *was* Laurence—returned to Vienna. I'm not sure I can get any more help from my friend to search for more detailed surveillance—from highway monitors and such. I just don't know if he has that kind of time and connections."

"Well, hell then—we're screwed. What else can we do?"

"Let's see what he can find out for us, okay? If he can't help, we'll just have to work with Interpol. Detective Cummings would need to contact the FBI and get them working with Interpol in Austria to start tracking down Laurence's movements there."

# Chapter 9

On the evening Laurence Kellerman had checked into the Hotel Bristol in Salzburg, he dined on roast pheasant, wild mushroom pudding, onion tart and red cabbage at the renowned hotel's Polo Lounge. Savoring a final sip of the Schloss Vollrad Riesling, he smacked his lips and signed the tab. Checking his watch, he picked up his briefcase and walked to the exit.

"Thank you, Heinz, wonderful dinner!" Laurence tipped the maître'd as he left the dining room, and walked across the lobby, taking the elevator to the conference room off the mezzanine to meet with Count Frederick von Strasser, who had arranged Laurence's accommodations under the fictitious name "John Hansen."

Laurence had met Count von Strasser four years earlier at a symposium featuring the biography and musical compositions of Mozart at the Mozarteum in Salzburg and again two years later at a similar gathering there. During their luncheon discussions, Laurence had been mesmerized by von Strasser's account of his acquisition and deaccession processes for rare books and fine art; he was especially impressed by von Strasser's intriguing stories of the contracts the count had negotiated. Laurence could not have known that von Strasser frequented such conferences to access potential targets for his clandestine terrorist group's pursuit of rare artifacts. When Laurence decided to return the Mozart Requiem Mass fragment to the Austrian National Library, Count von Strasser seemed like the ideal person to manage the transaction.

"Ah, Mr. Kellerman, good evening. So good to see you again, my friend! I trust you have found your accommodations acceptable."

"Quite so, count. Thank you for arranging it and for your generosity."

"At your service," said the count, bowing slightly. "This is my associate, Anton Sonntag, who will be assisting with our transaction."

"It's a pleasure, Mr. Sonntag." Laurence said, wondering at the associate's appearance. *Scarred right cheek, misshapen left ear, stocky build. A retired boxer, perhaps?*

"Please, gentlemen, let's sit down and get started."

They sat a table in front of a massive bookcase, its dozen shelves stacked with classic novels and the like, their colorful spines reflecting on the crystal goblets into which the count poured generous measures of Courvoisier. "Prosit!"

"Prosit!" both men responded.

"So, Laurence, I'm delighted that you could come here to finalize our arrangement," the count began. "Let's see ... the last time we discussed—"

"Count, I'm sorry, but I am here to tell you that the deal is off."

"What? Are you seriously saying, Mr. Kellerman, that you came all the way to Salzburg without bringing the fragment? That you have no intention whatsoever to proceed with our plan?" The tall, dark-haired middle-aged nobleman tilted his head slightly as he spoke, stroking his short-cropped, perfectly trimmed grey beard.

Laurence Kellerman gazed unflinchingly at the count. Outside the windows behind von Strasser, Laurence could see across the Salzach River to Old Town Salzburg—the mystical point in the universe where the genius of Johannes Chrysostomus Wolfgangus Theophilus Mozart entered this profane world. "Let me remind you, Count von Strasser," Laurence began, emphasizing each word, "that my sole reason for journeying here was to make certain that the Mozart fragment's final destination would be the Austrian National Library—to be reunited there with the original Requiem Mass autograph manuscript."

"Are you saying, sir, that you're not certain we can deliver on our promise to carry out this mission?" the retired boxer asked.

"I assure you, gentlemen, that I in no way mean any disrespect. However, there are serious questions that I must resolve before I can complete this transaction. I don't care if it means delaying this deal indefinitely, but I must be totally confident in the outcome."

"Mr. Kellerman," the count chafed, tugging at his red silk necktie, "I thought we had gone over the details repeatedly before you agreed to the terms. Isn't that why you're here right now?"

Laurence folded his hands on the table and fell silent, recalling his phone conversation with Oliver Yates just moments before getting off the plane in Salzburg that afternoon...

"Laurence! So glad I caught you. Have you met with von Strasser yet? I just received a tip that the count has no intention of delivering the Mozart fragment to the National Library, that he's arranged a meeting with a prospective purchaser."

"Your timing is impeccable as usual. I just got off my butt and am about to get off the plane."

"Laurence, you've got to find a way to kill this deal and get the hell out of there. Von Strasser is one of the principals in Ein Volk, a Neo-Nazi group based in Austria. Those goons are notorious for their scorched earth tactics. You're in real danger."

"Neo-Nazis! Okay, look, Oliver, we'll have to go with our back-up plan. Have your man meet me in my room at the Imperial tomorrow—I'll be there at one o'clock in the afternoon. Got it?"

"Okay. David Corbyn will meet you there. In the meantime, mate, please be quite wary of those gorillas down there."

"I'll do my best."

"... Mr. Kellerman?"

"Oh, yes. Sorry, count, but ... you see, I'm now uncertain that the way you plan to negotiate with the library will be successful. I've agreed to pay you one million dollars to complete this mission, and I must be certain that nothing will ... uh ... jeopardize this transaction and put the fragment—and my reputation—in danger. I am sure you can understand."

"No! I do *not* understand," the count retorted, his face turning red. "This has been the plan since our first communication, Mr. Kellerman. What has changed? What is your concern, sir?"

"I know damned well what we've discussed, Count von Strasser, but we're speaking here about an artifact containing the last words ever written in Mozart's hand—and it belongs to *me*. I, and I alone, will decide what happens to it. I cannot for one second be uncertain about the outcome. Can't you understand that, sir?"

"Of course I can! But what could possibly have changed? Let's go through the details again before—"

"No, I've made up my mind. The deal's off." Laurence rose from his seat. "I have several folks waiting for me in Vienna when I return tomorrow. I apologize for taking up so much of your time—but I hope you can understand my position."

"This is most distressing, Mr. Kellerman. For the past two months we've devoted an enormous amount of time and considerable expense planning the strategy and execution of this mission. And now—"

"Ah, certainly! I'm sure you've worked diligently, so I'm willing, of course, to compensate you for your efforts. We can finalize that matter tonight."

The count turned to his associate. "Draw up the figures for Mr. Kellerman to review, Anton, so we can settle this matter right now."

Laurence offered his hand in a gesture of good will.

The count stiffened. "Again, Mr. Kellerman, I think you're making a terrible mistake."

Laurence withdrew his hand. "Thank you, Count von Strasser."

Sonntag presented the requested invoice to the count for his review.

"I trust this figure will meet with your approval, Mr. Kellerman," said the count, handing the statement to Laurence.

When Laurence saw the six-figure amount, his eyebrows arched.

"Well, I guess I deserve this, don't I?"

He sat back down at the table, opened his briefcase, and fished out a certified bank check. Filling in the amount, he signed it with a flourish, removed the check, and handed it to the count.

"Exactly $250,000—as you requested, sir." *Not too small a price to pay to rescue the precious fragment, and my wrinkled old ass, from this godforsaken den of vipers.*

"Mr. Kellerman. I regret that we were unable to do business together."

"Another time, count. I'll be leaving for Vienna tomorrow morning."

"Of course, I'll have Anton get you to the airport with time to spare."

"That won't be necessary, count. I've already arranged my transportation. Good night, gentlemen." Von Strasser and Sonntag offered no departing words.

Back in his room, Laurence phoned Oliver.

"Laurence, are you all right, old man? What's happening down there?"

"I'm not sure, Oliver. I don't know if they bought my story, but it's cost me one hell of a price to find out. Anyway, I expect to be on that eight o'clock flight tomorrow morning. I'm planning to meet you and Corbyn as soon as I get back to Vienna to work out the rest of this fucked-up scheme. We'll see what happens."

"Just get out of there safe, mate. We'll take care of the rest at our end. Good luck, old chap. See you tomorrow afternoon."

※

After Laurence left the conference room, Count von Strasser and Anton Sonntag returned to the table. Von Strasser poured another round of brandy.

"What the hell is going on with that old geezer? Could he have gotten wind of our scheme? Is that what's queered this deal? Did he really come all the way here without bringing the fragment?"

Hunched over the table, Anton slurped his brandy, then looked up at his surly boss.

"Do you want me to send somebody up to Vienna to search his hotel room, count? Maybe he put the fragment in the private safe there. Every room at the Imperial has one."

"It's got to be there, Anton. We've got to get it, or I'll be answering to the cartel for this blunder. I can't afford to have this deal blow up on us."

Anton studied his boss's distressed face, just as countless times before he had probed those of the suspects he interrogated during his twenty years with the Special Task Force for Terrorist Activities. He didn't like what he saw.

"I don't believe I have any other recourse, Anton. Get hold of Rieger and tell him to go up there tonight. He's got to get into that hotel room before Laurence returns to Vienna tomorrow."

"Done!" Anton drained the goblet and hurried off. He could hear the empty glasses jingle to the pounding of the table by the infuriated count.

Sergeant Lukas Rieger had driven all night, arriving at the Hotel Imperial, in Vienna, at eight o'clock in the morning. A former employee of the federal police, the tall, stocky agent, nattily dressed in a dark blue suit, appeared relaxed despite the grueling five-hour drive. Before emerging from his white Mercedes Benz, Rieger pulled from his pocket the photograph of Laurence Kellerman that Anton Sonntag had given him before he left Salzburg. He studied it. *So, you're the old guy causing all this damned trouble and depriving me of my sleep.* Entering the hotel lobby, he marveled at the impeccably preserved tile floor, its vivid orange, yellow and brown colors reflecting the massive crystal chandelier overhead. He approached the desk clerk, who was about to leave following his overnight shift.

"Good morning, sir. How can I be of service?"

"*Guten Tag!* Could you please ring Mr. Laurence Kellerman's room? I have an urgent message for him."

"Certainly." The clerk reviewed the guest list, turned around and glanced at the key slots behind the desk. Kellerman's key was there. "Sorry, sir, but it appears that Mr. Kellerman is not in his room at this time."

The young sergeant grasped his chin, feigning distress. "Damn! Would you please call his room nonetheless—just to make certain?"

The clerk rang Laurence's room. "Sorry, sir, there's no answer."

"All right, thanks. Please see that he receives this message as soon as he returns. This is an urgent matter." Rieger handed the clerk a white envelope with Laurence Kellerman's name typed on it. He watched the clerk place it in the mail slot for room 435.

"Thank you," Rieger said, handing the clerk 20 Euros. "Oh, and which way to the men's room?"

"Thank *you*, sir. It's just across the lobby, to the right of the elevators."

"I appreciate your help. Good day."

"And you, too, sir." The clerk pocketed the generous tip. *Wonderful way to end the shift!*

Three minutes later, Sergeant Rieger was standing in front of Suite 435. Fishing a ghost keyset from his pocket, he found one that unlocked the door to Laurence Kellerman's room. After checking the hallway, he slowly opened the door. The early morning sun glowed through the bright red drapes covering the arched 12-foot-high windows. Stepping inside, he quietly closed the door behind him. Gripping the Glock 18 in his pocket, he turned on the overhead light and scanned the room, noting the location of the closet next to the bathroom. Rieger opened the bathroom door and flicked on the light, checking inside before moving to the closet. His pulse rate increased as he twisted the door handle, the anticipation thrilling him the same as the high in so many of his cases with the federal police. He opened the door. An overhead light automatically lit up the interior.

"Oh no!" He got down on one knee to inspect the impossible sight before him. The mangled door of the personal safe lay on the floor. With his index finger, Rieger traced the perimeter of the ravaged metal safe and charred wall, sniffing the deep brown stain it had deposited. "Dimethylbutane," he muttered. "They used a fucking plastic explosive to blow off the damned door!" He pulled a small flashlight out of his pocket and examined the inside of the safe.

"Nothing! The Count is gonna be pissed!" He stood up and began tapping the keys on his cell phone.

Laurence Kellerman finished shaving, then he dressed, packed his bag, and placed his briefcase on the bed. He savored a final bite of apple strudel from breakfast, washing it down with a splash of warm black coffee. He turned to the Bose clock radio—the same model as the one at home in his bedroom—and popped open its plastic casing, revealing the space from where he had removed the speaker. In an instant he was staring at the Mozart fragment, visible through the thin acrylic sleeve protecting it. *With the gestapo prowling about, one can't be careful enough.* He removed the relic from the radio and placed it into the leather pouch of his money belt, which he secured around his chest. Then he headed down to the lobby, and on to the airport. His plane to New York was leaving in two hours.

# Chapter 10

"What the hell are you saying, Rieger? Who else could have known about this?"

Count von Strasser paced the room in his pajamas, stretching the long phone line as far as it would go, knocking the lamp off the table.

"Listen, Rieger, I want you to follow Kellerman when he gets back to Vienna. Be sure he gets on that plane back to New York. Do you understand? I don't want him conning us here with some trick or tactic to throw us off."

"I'll stay right on him, count. Believe me, I'll make sure he doesn't give us the slip."

"Get back to me as soon as you have verified his departure. Understand, Rieger?"

"Right ... got it, I'll be in touch as soon as I've confirmed it. No problem, count."

"Good, sergeant," the count snapped, "I'll be waiting for your call."

Rieger looked back into the closet. "Wish I could see old Kellerman's face when he sees this shit!" He left the room and headed out to the pub he had spotted when arriving earlier, as good a place as any to set up a stake-out.

David Corbyn had served in MI6 for 35 years. Oliver Yates's closest friend and confidant, he often enjoyed martinis and dinner with him on weekends. Now approaching his 70th birthday, Agent Corbyn was still active with the Secret Intelligence Services. He worked out regularly and was physically fit. He continued styling his hair as he had done for decades: maintaining his reddish-brown color with generous portions of *Just for Men* hair dye. On this particular day, the seasoned detective entered the Hotel Imperial, nodded to the desk clerk, and headed for the elevator. Once inside room 435, he surveyed the scene, then checked the closet, finding exactly what he expected to see.

"Jolly decent job, those lads! Couldn't have done it better myself." He plumped down into an inviting balloon-back chair, resting his head against the silky soft cushioning, and faced the door. Half an hour later, a knock startled him awake. Corbyn stretched in the chair as the door opened.

"Ah, Oliver! You've finally made it," he yawned.

"David, I appreciate your taking on this gig at the last minute. The next round of Tanqueray martinis is on me, old chap. I have all the materials here in my briefcase, so let's get started."

"Work your magic, Oliver. The martinis can wait!"

Oliver Yates opened a duffle bag, removing four small plastic containers and a greyish-white wig. "How about sitting here, next to this floor lamp?"

"So, this stuff is going to get me a free trip to New York City, mate?"

"That's the least Her Majesty could do for you, David. And she's putting you up in the old Roosevelt Hotel."

"Hah! So generous of the old gal, though not exactly the Four Seasons that I was expecting."

They laughed as Oliver set to work.

"You may want to remove your shirt, my friend. I'll put a towel around you, but this can get a bit messy. We will start with the hair; that's the worst of it all. Let's work on those sideburns a bit. You've got to age about 10 years."

Corbyn winced when Oliver Yates applied the hair dye. "Phew! That junk smells worse than mine, old chap! Can hardly wait to shower."

"Sorry. Standard issue, you know."

After devouring his hearty European breakfast, a bloated Sergeant Rieger left the pub and ambled along the Kaernter Ring, stopping midway along the street to answer his cellphone.

It was the count.

"Is everything under control, Rieger?"

"Well, I just enjoyed a delightful breakfast and—"

"Okay, okay. We've just confirmed that Kellerman's boarded a flight to Vienna with an ETA of 11:45 this morning. Expect him to be arriving at the Imperial around 1300 hours."

"Copy that."

"He's booked on United Airlines flight 2640, departing for New York at 4:25 this afternoon. So, he'll be spending very little time in his hotel room before checking out. You need to keep your eyes on that hotel, Rieger. Be damned sure you follow him to the airport!"

"Yeah, I'm all set up. I've got a perfect spot for a bird's-eye view of the hotel entrance. And my car's parked in a spot next to the hotel, so I'll be right on him."

"Okay, sounds good. Remember, Rieger, call me to confirm that Kellerman has boarded the flight—and the exact time of its departure. Got that?"

"Yes, sir! I've got it," Rieger snapped.

"Good, I'll be waiting for your call."

"It will be my pleasure, Count von Strasser. Goodbye."

Rieger glanced at his watch. He had a couple of hours before Kellerman's arrival at the Imperial. The museums were opening, so he left the restaurant and headed for the center of the city. The Kunst Historisches Museum had been a favorite since he first visited Vienna with his family when he was eleven years old. It houses one of the world's greatest collections of armor—Rieger's longtime fascination. When he entered the museum, Rieger sighed. *Like coming home!* He hurried immediately to the salon that housed a wide array of 15th-century suits of armor—his favorite collection. He recalled his father explaining the craftsmanship that went into that formidable wartime attire—and its phenomenal advantage on the battlefield. It was only when he had wandered to the most remote salon that he thought to check his watch. "I'd better get my ass back there now," he muttered as he hurried out to the grand marble lobby.

Returning to the pub, Rieger selected a table at the window, facing the front entrance of the Hotel Imperial.

"So glad to see you again," said the waiter who had served him breakfast, Rieger's generous gratuity fresh in his mind.

" *'Gustav'* is it?"

"Thank you so much for remembering, sir."

"Good to be back, but I may have to leave in a hurry when business calls."

"Very good, sir. What can I get you?"

Rieger glanced at the menu.

"A tall Dortmunder and a Brats sandwich, please."

"Right away, sir."

Across the street in room 435, Oliver Yates was putting the finishing touches on his makeover of David Corbyn. Stepping back, Oliver assessed his work, holding a photograph of Laurence Kellerman next to David. "It's quite frightening!" he exclaimed. "Eerie in a way—you look just like the old man!"

"Well, hells bells, Oliver, isn't that why your pay scale is so damned high?"

"Right you are, old mate." Oliver tweaked David's left cheek, strategically placing a plastic mole on it—a final touch of authenticity. "Now let's hope the old boy makes it here in one piece."

Sergeant Rieger had just taken the last bite of the Bratwurst sandwich and was hoisting his glass to drain the final ounce of his second German brew when he saw the airport limousine arriving at the hotel's front entrance.

*12:55—that could be our boy!* Rieger fished the photograph of Kellerman out of his jacket pocket, holding it in front of him. As the limo driver opened the door, Rieger moved closer to the window, from where he observed an elderly, somewhat white-haired gentleman in a grey suit turn to the driver and hand him a gratuity.

*Got him!*

At the front desk, Laurence Kellerman checked in, asking for his key.

"Ah, Mr. Kellerman, wonderful to have you back," the desk clerk responded, handing him a white envelope. "An urgent message left in your mailbox, sir."

"Very good, thank you. I'll be checking out in about an hour or so, so I'll need the limo to the airport, please."

"Not a problem, sir. Call when you're ready."

Laurence headed to the elevator and up to his room. He turned the key slowly and opened the door.

"Laurence, old chap—you made it!" Oliver Yates cried out.

"So good to see you, my friend." Peering over Oliver's shoulder as they hugged, Laurence was staring at a mirror image of himself seated in a chair across the room. "Who the hell is *that*?"

"Laurence Kellerman, meet Laurence Kellerman," Oliver said.

"Poor chap!" Laurence quipped. "You look exactly like me!"

Laurence held up the white envelope he received from the desk clerk. "An urgent message awaiting me on my return." He opened it, unfolding the paper inside. "Blank, of course—not even a swastika printed on it. So, I suppose you two fellows are not the first to have entered this room since I left three days ago, right?"

"Well, it worked, old chap. We blew the door off the safe before they got here, and I believe they fell for it. But we don't have much time, Laurence," Oliver cautioned. "I've booked you into room 336, under the name 'Samuel Allison.' Here's your new passport and airline ticket. You'll be leaving for New York tomorrow afternoon at 4:25."

" '*Samuel Allison,*' you say? My second name in two days! Well, I've been called a hell of a lot worse!"

"Here's what's happening, Laurence. You've got to get out of those clothes so David can maintain the appearance of you that the surveillant observed."

"I'm afraid they're a bit wrinkled and raunchy, my friend," Laurence said.

"Not to worry," Oliver replied. "I'll tidy them up a bit. And that luggage?—I assume you were carrying that on your way into the hotel?"

"Yes," Laurence answered.

"David's got to carry that out with him when he leaves."

Laurence placed the suitcase on the desk, transferring its contents to the black leather Tumi suitcase that Oliver provided. "Okay, I've got to wash up before changing into this new outfit. I'll be right back." He appeared ten minutes later, refreshed and dapper in khaki trousers, light blue, button-down shirt, and dark blue sports jacket. He slipped into a pair of neatly buffed cordovan loafers.

"Quite smart, Laurence!" Oliver observed. "Are we all set, then, gentlemen?"

"Good to go, Oliver," David Corbyn responded.

"Watch your back, David. We'll have someone at the boarding gate to make sure you get on that flight with no problem. Okay, mate?"

"Roger that, Oliver."

Laurence shook hands with David, marveling again at his uncanny resemblance.

"Thank you for taking on this risky task, David. It's an incredibly urgent matter for me. I trust our paths will cross again."

"Hopefully, you'll recognize me should that occur," David joked.

"I'm not sure how that would be possible, my friend. You'll no longer be my twin, but give me a shout-out if you happen to see me first!"

Oliver Yates squeezed David Corbyn's arm. "Do be careful, old chum."

"Good working with you chaps. See you after my holiday, Oliver."

The trio separated. Laurence moved down to room 336.

"I'll be bunking next door, Laurence," Oliver said. "As soon as we get the all-clear, we'll execute the next step in our plan— getting you home safely. So, let's sit tight for now until David arrives in New York."

"Sounds good, Oliver. Do you want to have dinner this evening?"

Oliver hesitated. "Sorry, Laurence, I've got … uh, several items to deal with before tomorrow afternoon. I've got to get started on them tonight. But I've taken the liberty to book a table at eight tonight for Samuel Allison at Opus, downstairs. I'll check in with you in the morning."

"Much appreciated, Oliver. Sorry you can't join me."

Thanks so much. Enjoy, old friend. But please keep that fragment in your safe whenever you leave your room. You can't be too careful with all those thugs lurking about."

"You know I will, Oliver."

David Corbyn checked out at the front desk.

"Mr. Kellerman, your limousine is ready."

"Thank you."

As David Corbyn stepped outside the hotel, Lukas Rieger spotted him. A mumbled *Wiedersehen* to the waiter was all that remained in the air above the tumbled chair left behind as Rieger dashed from the pub. Within seconds he was in his Mercedes, easing the car forward as the black limousine carrying Laurence Kellerman's doppelganger pulled away from the hotel.

David Corbyn emerged from the limo at the United Airlines gate forty minutes later. Rieger left his Mercedes with the valet, all the while keeping his subject in sight.

As he entered the airport, Rieger followed. After lunch at the Café Wien, David made his way to Gate D38, Rieger trailing ten yards behind.

When the airline announced the departing flight to New York's Kennedy Airport, David took a deep breath, fished a passport and boarding pass out of his suit pocket and presented them to the attendant.

"Thank you, Mr. Kellerman, we hope you have a pleasant trip home."

Just a few yards away at this point, Rieger heard the greeting and saw its recipient board the plane. Returning to the lounge, he waited until the plane had departed, half an hour later. Then he called Count von Strasser.

Later that evening, Laurence undressed. He removed the money belt from around his chest and opened it, pulling out the acrylic receptacle harboring the Mozart fragment. He gazed at it for a few minutes, reprising the ritual he had so often performed in his den. He put it back in the money belt and placed it back in the safe. He closed the door and entered the combination on the panel and tugged at the handle, making certain that it was secure. Then he showered, dressed, and left for the Opus Restaurant downstairs.

Returning to his room after dinner, before going to bed, Laurence opened the closet door in his room, tugged at the handle of the safe making sure it was secure. "Sleep safe, Mr. Mozart."

# Chapter 11

"Ten o'clock, already? I must have overslept!" Lawrence dialed room service.

A half hour later, he finished the rye toast and poached eggs, and was sipping the last drops of coffee. "Okay, let's get this bag of bones together and get the hell out of here," he muttered.

Showered and partially dressed, Laurence opened his luggage and carefully stacked his clothes inside.

Snapping shut the black Tumi bag that Oliver had given him, he walked to the closet and opened the door. Getting down on one knee, he punched in the code and opened the safe, pulling out the money belt. "Good morning, Mr. Mozart!" He placed the money belt on the desk and opened it. Nothing inside. Frantically running his fingers along the inside of the belt, he cried out, "Empty! Empty! Empty!" Laurence grabbed the phone, punching in 3-3-8. He could hear the ringing next door in Oliver Yates's room. Nobody answered. He slammed the phone back onto its cradle, picked it up and dialed again. No response. He bolted out of his room and pounded on Oliver's door. No response. Back in his room, he dialed the front desk.

"Hello, this is, uh, Samuel Allison in room 336. Please ring Mr. Yates in room 338."

"Yes sir, Mr. Allison."

A moment later the clerk responded, "Sorry, Mr. Allison, there's no answer— Oh, one moment! I see that Mr. Yates has checked out."

"Are you sure? When?"

"Yes, Mr. Allison—last evening, sir."

"Is there a message for me?"

68

"No sir. No messages at all."

Laurence slammed the phone down and collapsed onto the chair. "You set me up, Oliver!" he screamed. *"Why? Why? Why?"*

The previous evening, Oliver Yates had waited next door until he heard Laurence leaving his room for dinner. Twenty minutes later, peering into the dimly lit Opus Restaurant, Yates spotted Laurence at the table in the back corner he had reserved for him. "Great!" he whispered. Returning to the third floor, he slipped into Laurence's room using a pass key. Seconds later, crouching on the closet floor, he removed a magnetic scanner from his coat pocket and positioned it over the keyboard on the front panel of the safe. He pressed a small button on its face. A red light began blinking until digits 6-26-12-5-91 flashed on the tiny keyboard screen. After two short beeps, the door of the safe popped open. Oliver reached inside, grabbed the money belt and closed the safe, returning the scanner to his coat pocket. He placed the money belt on the desk and carefully removed the acrylic vessel, contemplating its precious contents. "Marvelous … marvelous!" The veteran MI6 agent placed the fragment in his inside jacket pocket, returning the money belt to the safe and locking it. Then he checked out of the hotel. Fifteen minutes later he was in a taxi speeding across the city along Weiskirchner Strasse on his way to a pension hotel near the University of Applied Arts. He had become close friends with Al and Eva Froede, the owners of the hotel, early in his career. He and his wife had stayed there often on their visits to Vienna. And Oliver, even when alone, stayed there whenever he traveled to the city on assignment.

A million contradictory thoughts were crashing through Laurence's brain as his grip on the arms of the chair tightened.

"Yates—you traitor!"

Six months earlier, Laurence had met with Oliver Yates while vacationing in London. He confided in his longtime friend about one of the most problematic decisions he had ever made in his life. During the past 24 years, gazing at the Mozart Requiem Mass fragment had become a religious experience for him—conjuring up the glorious memories from his youth upon discovering the unearthly majesty of the composer's music. The cherished fragment also invoked the sadness of the funeral Masses following the unbearable deaths of his parents and his beloved wife, Gayle. By his 80th birthday, Laurence's concern for the future of the Mozart fragment had intensified. *Who can I trust to honor the value of this magnificent artifact? I can't risk having any harm come to it.*

While listening to a performance of the Mozart Requiem Mass at St. James Church in Manhattan during the previous Holy Week, Laurence decided to reunite the fragment with its autograph manuscript at the Austrian National Library in Vienna. Count von Strasser had been the only person Laurence deemed competent enough to manage the transaction for him. *How can I ever get it back there now?*

Laurence glanced at his watch.

"I've got to get out of here."

He dialed the front desk.

"Hello. Samuel Allison, here. I'm about to check out and I need transportation to the airport."

Laurence gazed around the room, as if standing on an empty stage, the wounded sole survivor in a Wagnerian opera. He pulled his cellphone out of his pocket and punched in Arthur Keyes' phone number.

# Chapter 12

It had been the latest in a long string of sleepless nights for Arthur Keyes. Haunting scenarios continued to rattle him every time he closed his eyes. *Where could Laurence be? Is the old guy okay? And the Mozart fragment—is it safe?* He finally dozed off—only to be awakened by his cellphone. His arm shot out aimlessly, his hand flailing on the nightstand for the phone, knocking it onto the floor. Fumbling successfully for the light, he turned it on and picked up the phone.

"Hello? Hello?"

"Arthur?"

"Laurence! Is that you, Laurence? Are you okay? Where the hell are you?"

"You're not gonna believe what's going on, Art. I'm still in Vienna, but I've got to get the hell out of here. I'm leaving for New York shortly. Can you pick me up at Kennedy? I'm arriving at 12:40 tomorrow morning, United flight 8841."

"United 8841, okay, got it. I'll be there, Laurence. Is there anything you need?"

"Wait 'til you find out!"

"Whatever. See you tomorrow morning. Be safe!"

*Should I contact Leopold and fill him in on this? Linn could …no, no. I gotta be the one who picks him up and gets him home safely. Then we'll decide what's best. What's he gonna do when he finds out that I've revealed the whole damned story?* He sauntered into the bathroom to prepare for the long, grueling day that lay ahead.

At the office he told his secretary to hold all his calls and refuse meetings for the rest of the day. He imagined the torturous trip to

Kennedy and, worse, the backbreaking ride returning to the city. Worst of all, he imagined Laurence's reaction to his decision to involve Leopold in the entire Mozart conundrum. *He's gonna fucking kill me when I tell him. I just know it!* Throughout the day his voicemail logged more than twenty messages—many from Linn anxiously trying to find out what was going on with him and his sudden unavailability. Three messages from Leopold showed that he had vital information to relate about Oliver Yates, whom Leopold had mentioned frequently in their conversations. Arthur listened to the messages on his phone, pulling him in opposite directions. *No way! I can't respond to them now. I gotta get the old man back and let him decide what he wants to do next.*

Arthur arrived at Kennedy Airport at 11:30 that evening. He steered his grey metallic BMW X6 up to the parking space he had reserved earlier that afternoon at the Special Needs location closest to the United Airlines terminal. *I'm gonna make damned sure no freakin' look-alike gets off the plane this time! It better be Laurence, or I am getting on the next flight to Timbuktu!*

Just after midnight, Arthur entered the waiting area outside Customs in Terminal 8's Concourse B. The airline had posted Flight 8841 as "12:40 ON TIME from Vienna."

After stopping for a Starbucks double shot espresso, Arthur perched on a long metal bench as close to the exit from Customs as he could find. *Who the hell knows how long the cockamamie reentry ritual will drag on?* He sipped the strong Arabica brew, but finding little help from it, dozed off within ten minutes. Awakened forty-five minutes later by the announcement of the arrival of Flight 8841, he shot up from his seat. Squinting, he shielded his eyes from the harsh fluorescent light above, straining to focus on the rumpled passengers trickling out of the processing center, mumbling to one another as they toddled by.

A familiar shock of disheveled greyish-white hair appeared in the doorway yards away. The old man shuffling forward seemed tired and lost.

"Over here, Laurence!" Arthur called out. *"Laurence!"* he yelled again, louder, attempting to snap his boss out of the brain-numbing semi-consciousness that a one o'clock a.m. slog through customs checkpoint inflicts on its victims.

Laurence finally saw him and began maneuvering his way through the escaping crowd. "Thank God you were able to come, Art!"

Arthur took Laurence's bag in his left hand, wrapping his right arm around his mentor's back.

"Laurence, I'm so damned glad you made it back safe."

"Yeah, but if I had to answer one more inane question about my trip from that fascist Customs agent, you'd be visiting me in a federal prison!"

"Okay, Laurence, let's get you home safe."

※

By the time they arrived at Laurence's apartment, it was already past three o'clock. Laurence surveyed his living room, taking in the familiar, reassuring sight and aromas, basking in the welcome comfort that coming home after a long journey bestows on weary travelers.

"Laurence, there's a few urgent items I've got to talk to you about. When you disappeared and I couldn't figure out where—"

Laurence placed his hand on Arthur's shoulder, stopping him mid-sentence. "It's late, Art, and I'm exhausted. I'm going to take a quick shower and collapse into the bed I've been yearning for all week long. Whatever you have can wait until later. I'll call you when I've gotten myself back together. Okay, son?" He grasped Arthur's shoulder again, caressing it. "Thanks for being here for me."

"Certainly, of course, Laurence. Get a good rest. You sure as hell seem like you need it."

Arthur walked slowly to the elevator, torn by the comforting feeling of knowing that Laurence was safe at home, but wary of the intense drama that loomed.

# Chapter 13

Linn awoke at 5:30 and ambled to the kitchen to brew her dad's favorite blend of Lavazza Espresso. She began mixing the pancake batter as the sausages cooked when she heard the door to her dad's bedroom open.

"Dad are you up?" she sang out. No answer. "Dad?"

Leopold rounded the corner from the hallway, and stopped, leaning against the wall to catch his balance as he rubbed his forehead. "Good morning, honey," he mumbled.

Hearing her dad's voice, Linn turned away from the stove. He looked pale as he entered the kitchen —and lost his balance again.

"Dad, are you okay? You don't look so good."

"Oh, I've had this damned headache all night. It just seems to be getting worse. It can't possibly be from that spectacular *St. Emilion* we had at dinner last night," he joked half-heartedly.

"Come to the table and sit down, dad. I've got some hot coffee ready for you." She poured the hot brew into a mug and placed it on the table. His hands were trembling as he grabbed the mug, startling Linn. "You don't look well *at all*, dad. Is this something new—your shaking?"

Leopold closed his eyes for a moment, before responding.

"Just like your mother! Always fussing about."

"Come on, dad. Don't go pulling that *Just like your mother* routine again. Something's not right with you. I noticed yesterday afternoon that you seemed unusually tired. And now this shaking. I think we should get you over to the doctor today and have her check you out."

"See? There you go again! Doctor this, doctor that."

74

"Seriously, you're going to be traveling back to Brussels in a few days, and I think you should get checked out before you go. It can't hurt." She sat down next to him, placing her hand on his arm. "Please, dad, do it just to be safe. Okay?"

"How about some of those sausages? They smell so damned good. Are you just tormenting me with them?"

Linn touched his neck as she got up.

"Dad, you're burning up! You have a fever. That does it! After breakfast we're going to see Dr. Ricker."

Leopold slid his chair away from the table, raising his arms high in surrender.

"Okay, okay, I'll do it, but how about some sausages first? *Feed* a fever, starve a cold— right?"

"That's *not* how mom used to put it!" Linn laughed, as she forked two sausages onto his plate.

Dr. Ann Ricker had been Linn's primary care physician for the past eight years. They had become close friends, and occasionally had dinner or enjoyed a show together. Like Linn, Dr. Ricker was a career-driven professional who devoted her life to her work. She, too, had never married. She and Linn often confided in one another, at times commiserating about their problems. Linn was the solitary support for Dr. Ricker after her father was killed in an automobile accident. She had no siblings, and an untreatable cancer claimed her mother's life shortly after Dr. Ricker had completed her medical internship at Johns Hopkins University—all before her father's sudden death.

After scheduling the doctor's appointment for ten o'clock that morning, Linn notified the office that she would be arriving later in the day.

He had been asleep for less than four hours, but Arthur awoke at eight o'clock, consumed a cup of Keurig-blended Donut Shop coffee, dressed, and headed out the door in an hour. When he got to his office, he asked his secretary to call Linn Beckers and have her come right over.

"I'm sorry, Mr. Keyes, but Linn hasn't gotten in yet. She called about half an hour ago to say she had an important stop to make before coming in."

"Damn it, Cynthia! Have her call me as soon as she gets in."

Arthur sat at his desk, staring blankly at the wall. It was impossible to concentrate on clients and contracts. This Mozart problem must be resolved, and he must somehow rescue Laurence from this ordeal. *I'll go review this endless drama with Linn and Leopold before I see the old man. Who knows what state Laurence will be in this morning?*

The buzzing intercom brought him back to why he was in the office in the first place.

"Call from Mr. Bloomberg, Mr. Keyes."

"Cynthia, could you, uh, no—never mind, put him through. Thanks."

Arthur struggled through the conversation with one of his top clients, nearly forgetting the impending court date. After he hung up, he pushed the intercom button.

"Cynthia, no more calls, please. Just let me know when Linn gets in." Arthur continued in his zombie-like trance, finally dozing off as he waited Linn's arrival.

※

After Dr. Ricker examined Leopold, she spoke with Linn while her father dressed in the room next door.

"I've ordered a CT scan and some blood tests. Your dad can get them downstairs before you leave."

"Why? What is it, Ann? What did you find?"

"Your dad complained of having headaches recently. And since he's experiencing some trembling in his right hand—and said he's been feeling a bit dizzy lately—I want to run some tests to see if he might be suffering from some type of brain aneurysm or tumor. I think we should play it safe."

"Of course. Thanks, Ann. I'll get him down there right away."

"The tests won't take long; you'll be out in no time. They'll send the results directly to me. I'll call you as soon as I hear anything."

Leopold walked in as Linn and Dr. Ricker were finishing. "Aha!—a conspiracy. I knew it!"

"Okay, Mr. Detective," his daughter quipped, "let's get you to the lab."

After Leopold's tests, he and Linn took a taxi home. Back in her apartment she hugged him. "Dad, I'm so glad you agreed to let Dr. Ricker check you out."

"Me too! It's been a long time since a lovely young woman's handled my body so delicately."

"Glad to hear her magic touch has you feeling better already! But I've got to check in with the office. Are you going to be okay here alone?"

"Shoo! Go to work. Don't let your old man screw up your career."

"There's some chicken salad in the fridge and a loaf of—"

"Ta, ta, ta... am I a child who can't find the refrigerator? Go! Get back to work. I'll be fine." He kissed her forehead. "Thanks for taking care of your old man."

"Okay. I'll check on you later. Try to take a nap. Maybe you'll get some strength back."

"Get on your way before they fire you, Miss Nightingale!"

# Chapter 14

"Okay, CJ, you'd better finish packing. You know how screwed up I-95 to the airport can be."

Jeff was more nervous than Christopher. His son was about to embark on the first leg of what promised to be a magnificent career. Jeff's transformation from wild youth to doting father had surprised him as much as his friends. *I never dreamed I would have a kid with such talent. I guess I must have done something right along the way—as impossible as that is to believe.* He recalled the countless number of times Heinrich Winterbottom had criticized him for his carousing and drug use. *"Don't you think you should grow up, Jeff? You're 30 years old but take no responsibility for anything!"* On and on he'd go.

Christopher's cell phone buzzed.

"Excuse me, is this the famous Christopher Jeffrey Lambert?" asked the mischievous voice of Matthew Stephenson, breaking Christopher's tension.

"Sorry, you must have punched in the wrong number," Christopher laughed. "This is a foundling troubadour about to stick his neck out to the world."

"Yes, my esteemed nephew's about to wow the concert stages of Europe!"

"Well, I, um, I've just finished packing and we're about to leave for Philly International."

"Don't let me keep you, kid. Leo and I just want to say, 'Break a leg'—*no fingers*—just a leg, okay? And don't forget, we'll be joining everyone in Brussels for your final concert. We've already booked

78

Uncle Ricky's favorite restaurant in all of Belgium. Cheers! See ya soon!"

"You dudes are amazing. I can hardly wait!"

Christopher's mother had retrieved their car and was waiting in the driveway below their condominiums as he and his dad exited the lobby. They piled into the Lexus and set off to see Christopher make his mark in the music world.

# Chapter 15

"Good morning," her secretary said as Linn entered the office. "Mr. Keyes asked that you see him as soon as you get in. He seems a bit, uh, *distracted* this morning."

"Thanks for the heads-up, Cindy. I'll be there in a minute."

As soon as she saw Arthur's face, Linn knew something was wrong, his loosened tie adding to her suspicion.

"Everything okay, Linn?"

"Yeah, I'm all right, but dad's had some odd symptoms this morning, so I took him to the doctor."

"Nothing serious, I hope. I don't want to worsen things with all of the crap I've got to run by him."

"He'll be fine, Art. I'm certain he would welcome any intrigue you want to spin with him. But what's going on with *you*, Art?"

Arthur took a deep breath, exhaling his response: "Laurence is back ..."

Linn rose halfway up from her chair. "What? Where's he been? When did he—?"

"Last night," Arthur said. He recounted the gruesome early morning details, reliving the ordeal again.

"Unbelievable! This craziness must be screwing up Laurence's mind totally. What are we going to do?"

"I'm hoping your dad has some suggestions on how to start unravelling this insane situation. It's way beyond anything Laurence can do to resolve it on his own."

Linn thought for a moment. "What about coming for dinner tonight? We can talk this over with dad. Maybe ..."

Arthur's phone rang. "Damn it!—"*What*, Cindy?"

"Sorry, Mr. Keyes, I know you said to hold your calls, but Mr. Kellerman is on the line."

"Put him through!"

Holding his hand over the phone, he mimed *Laurence* to Linn. She got up to leave, but Arthur waved her back.

"How are you this morning, Laurence? Were you able to get some rest?"

"Slept like a baby! Nothing like a couple of snorts of Maker's Mark to calm one down! I want you to come over so we can explore ways to deal with this *mishigas*."

"I'll be right there."

"Thanks, son. I'll see you when you get here."

"Linn, the old man has no idea I've told anyone about this Mozart scheme. He's gonna freak out when I lay this on him—on top of everything else!"

"Listen, Art, you know he has profound respect for my dad. It may help him to know that someone with dad's background, contacts and expertise can help him."

"Well, I'd better get over there and light the fuse. I'll call you after the explosion—if I'm still able to talk!"

One look at Laurence in the doorway of his apartment was enough to know something tragic had happened since he saw him earlier that day. Despite Laurence's calm demeanor—and his pleasant, cheerful phone conversation— his usually placid, self-assured visage appeared troubled and older, his wrinkles deeper.

"Thanks for coming over so quickly, Art. Let's get a cup of coffee from the kitchen."

Laurence's words, ordinarily flowing smoothly, were now halting.

"Art ... son ... something profoundly unnerving occurred in Vienna, and ... for the first time I can ever remember, ... I'm at a total loss as to how to deal with it. You're the only person I've trusted with this saga about how my fascination with Mozart led me to acquire that precious Requiem fragment. But now ... I've lost it! *It's gone, Art! I have no hope of ever seeing it again.*"

"How did that ever happen? You've always guarded it with your life."

"That's why I had you come. It's a long, ridiculous tale."

"Well, Laurence, I've got something to tell *you* that *I've* done. And I hope you'll understand why I had to do it."

The old man's back stiffened and his eyes widened, anticipating a revelation. Arthur recounted the actions he had taken when he heard about Laurence's rendezvous with the Neo-Nazi cabal—how he had involved Linn's father and the NYPD chief. When finished, he braced himself for the firestorm he expected. Laurence shrugged. "Son, that's exactly what I would've expected you to do. Why do you think I trusted you with my secret? I've been flummoxed by Oliver Yates, a longtime friend. He's the one who stole the Mozart fragment from me."

"We just might be able to get some information about that. Linn's dad has recently retired and is here on vacation. He's been contacting friends at law enforcement agencies in Salzburg and Vienna. I just learned from Linn this morning that he's got up-to-date information to report and—"

"Hell then," Laurence interrupted, "let's get him here and find out what he's learned!"

Arthur was already on his cellphone.

"Hi, Linn! Is it possible for you and your dad to come to Laurence's place today? There's some really serious shit going down. Laurence and I are hoping to hell that what your dad's found out might help us figure out what to do next."

"Of course, Art. Dad has a follow-up appointment with Dr. Ricker later this afternoon, but we can be there around six."

# Chapter 16

Oliver Yates sat alone in his familiar, two-star pension bedroom in Vienna, wide awake at three o'clock in the morning—exhausted and overwhelmed with guilt. He had just betrayed the best friend he ever had so he could avenge the ghosts of his father. Esteemed Masons in London, father and son had devoted their lives to the welfare of their Masonic Lodge, established a century earlier primarily for police and law enforcement officers. When a group of Nazis stormed their lodge during World War II, Oliver's grandfather suffered a concussion, resulting in brain damage leading to his early retirement from the police force. Oliver never forgot how his grandfather struggled with aphasia and depression during the last years of his life.

Oliver had been furious when he learned from the Secret Intelligence Service—just hours before Laurence's meeting with Count von Strasser in Salzburg—that the count was not, in fact, planning to return the Mozart fragment to the Austrian government, as Laurence had believed. He was even more enraged to hear that the count was the head of a Neo-Nazi cell that was plotting to obtain the fragment from Laurence in order to sell it to help finance their political and terrorist activities in Europe. Oliver vowed to stop them, even if it meant losing his best friend. When he learned how the Neo-Nazis had tricked Laurence into believing their intentions were legitimate, Oliver Yates knew he couldn't rely on Laurence to return the fragment to the Austrian National Library. *I've got to get it back there myself!*

In the morning, Oliver walked to Saint Stephen's Cathedral, Austria's iconic temple of Christianity. He proceeded to the side altar where the stark funeral mass for Wolfgang Amadeus Mozart had been so unceremoniously and hurriedly conducted early in the freezing morning of December 5, 1791. *How terrible that his death was treated so callously—this genius who composed the most celebrated Mass for the Dead!*

Still not fully awake, Oliver knelt at the very altar at which Mozart's mass had been celebrated. "So help me God," he whispered, "I vow to restore the great dignity to his legend."

Oliver left the cathedral and hurried along the Kohlmarkt to the perennially popular iconic Café der Demel, where he met with his friend Franz Beitzel, assistant director general of the Austrian National Library. The National Library housed the Mozart Requiem Mass autograph manuscript—minus the fragment in Oliver's possession. Beitzel had served five years as a field investigator for the Austrian Federal Police before earning a doctorate in library science and research, leading to a position with the Austrian government. Within five years he was promoted from a senior research assistant to the post of director of acquisitions before his appointment to assistant general director. He and Oliver Yates had met at a cyber surveillance symposium in Vienna. Beitzel had helped Oliver often during the past seven years as he sought connections to data involving his investigations.

"Ah, *Danke*," he said as the waiter seated him in a corner table by the window facing the Graben. When Franz Beitzel entered the café he saw Oliver seated near the door. They hugged. "So good to see you, Franz!"

"So, what's the marvelous occurrence bringing us together after—what? seven years already?"

"Hold on, Franz. How about a couple of those miraculous confections before we get into all that? What will you have, my friend?"

"Well, apfelstrudel, of course! And a cappuccino."

Oliver looked at the waiter. "The Sachertorte, for me," he said, "and a double espresso, please."

Franz studied his friend's face, remembering the grim times Oliver had suffered after his wife's death. He looked tired—exhausted.

"So, what's going on with you, Oliver?" Franz began.

"When I tell you why I am here, you'll never be the same person again as long as you live."

"Well! I hope I'm not the subject in one of your MI6 international intrigues, man," Franz said, half joking, half probing.

Before Oliver could answer, the waiter returned with their order.

Oliver touched his espresso to Franz's cappuccino. "To old friends!"

"Prosit!"

Oliver hadn't taken even a sip of his espresso before blurting out, "Franz, whatever happened to that Mozart Requiem Mass Autograph fragment that disappeared from the Brussels Expo '58?"

"*Gott im Himmel*, Oliver! Why the devil would you ask me a question like that—out of the clear blue Vienna sky?"

Oliver laughed heartily at his friend's reaction, drawing a split second of silence from the powder-sugared visages of several surrounding gourmands.

"Sorry, Franz, please don't choke on those yummy apple morsels."

"Well, hell, why would you ambush a guy with such a question?"

"I recently read a story in *The Times* about a theory claiming the stolen fragment had been sold on the black market to some billionaire Mozart fanatic in the states."

"I'm afraid I missed *that* tale. You know, there's been so many theories about that travesty spun out over the past six decades, one can hardly keep up with all of them. So, what was the upshot? Who's this billionaire connoisseur supposed to be?"

"I don't know who the person is. But I know where the fragment is!"

Franz pushed away from the table. "Stop, Oliver! Stop right there. We can't be having this conversation. There's a hot investigation going on right now in pursuit of recent tips the government's received. I ... I can't be discussing this with you right now. I apologize, my friend, but—"

"*Recent tips?*" Oliver's eyeballs were bulging.

"Settle down, Oliver! Let's get together at your place tonight. I'll go over some of the things I've heard—just between us friends."

"*Wunderbar*, Franz! I am staying at a pension I've enjoyed for years. Amelia loved it, too."

Oliver turned the pink cocktail napkin over, slipped a pen out of his pocket and jotted down the address.

"Around seven?"

"Very good! See you then. I've got to get back to the office."

They got up and shook hands, neither speaking a final word. Oliver watched his friend leave the legendary palace of confections, and sat back down, feeling relieved. *Finally, I'll resolve this problem and have the Mozart fragment returned to its rightful place of honor.*

On the way back to his office, Franz Beitzel took out his cellphone. "Hello, count. I've just got some important info about our project ...Yes, yes ... I'll get back to you later tonight."

As he left the café and made his way along the Graben, Oliver Yates decided it was time to reveal his plan to the one person who needed to know. He sat on a bench, shaded by a billowy overhead umbrella, pulled out his phone and called Laurence.

※

After four hours tossing and turning, Laurence had just dozed off when his cellphone awoke him. It took him a few seconds to realize he was at home in his own bedroom.

"Kellerman here. Who is it?"

"Laurence, old chap, is that really you?"

"Is this the worst fucking nightmare I've ever had, or could this possibly be Oliver Judas Yates?"

"I'm afraid the nightmare is all mine, old friend. I'm praying with all my heart and soul that you'll forgive me for what I've done."

"Have you finally lost your mind, Oliver?"

"Hold on, Laurence. I waited until David Corbyn told me that you had returned to New York safely. So then I—"

By now, Laurence was out of bed, bellowing into the phone. "How terribly kind of you to show such concern for your best friend—who you just robbed of his greatest possession on earth!"

"Yes! Yes! You've got every right to loathe me. I deserve the full force of your hatred for what I have done. But, please, Laurence, give me a few minutes to explain."

"That would be too damned generous," Laurence replied, "but go ahead and try."

In a fast, high-pitched review, Oliver ran through his effort to assist with the return of the Mozart fragment to the Austrian National Library with the help of his trusted friend Franz Beitzel. "You see, I'm really just trying to help you, Laurence," he concluded.

"Why in God's name didn't you tell me about your idea, Yates? We could have discussed it. You should have at least given me the option. What happens now?"

"The fragment's safe, Laurence. I'll be handing it over to Beitzel this evening. He's the assistant general director of the library. He'll make sure it's reunited with the Mozart manuscript tomorrow morning. God, I hope you can somehow forgive me for this terrible transgression."

"Well, I don't know about God, but *for me* that would be one hell of a stretch!"

"I understand, Laurence, believe me. I'll call you tomorrow as soon as I've confirmed that the library has received the treasure."

Laurence sat on the edge of the bed, struggling with his contradicting emotions, angry at his friend, but relieved that the problem he had tried to resolve for years was finally about to end.

"Oliver ... you damn well better call me the instant you've confirmed it, or I'm coming after you, wherever the hell you are!"

"Sorry to have gotten your dander up so early in the morning, old chap."

"I'm going back to bed now, Oliver. Get the hell off my phone!"

Sitting in bed, thousands of miles away, the tired octogenarian, in his pajamas, laughed at the absurdity of his own threatening words.

# Chapter 17

"Leopold, so terrific seeing you again!—and Linn, as always—welcome! Thanks for interrupting your vacation on such short notice."

"Ah, you're always part of my holiday in New York, Laurence. No visit here would be complete without seeing you. And thanks, Art, for bringing us all together tonight." His impish smile drew hearty laughs from everybody.

"So, everyone—let's have some refreshments!" The four of them settled into two snow-white sofas on opposite sides of a magnificent, dark green marble fireplace, Laurence and Arthur in one, Leopold and Linn in the other. A huge bouquet of yellow irises (Brussels' native flower) encircled by dozens of red poppies (the national flower) adorned the massive glass-covered cocktail table between the sofas. Laurence's caterer had surrounded the exotic display with an assortment of hors d'oeuvres: colossal shrimp, mini quiches, lobster claws, Stilton cheese, and beef filets encroute. Cabernet Sauvingon, Pouilly Fume and Moet Chandon champagne completed the buffet.

"Laurence, you're truly amazing, my friend—greeting me with flowers from my homeland," Leopold said.

"Yes, they're gorgeous! How very thoughtful!" Linn added.

"The least I could do," Laurence replied. "Please, help yourselves, everyone. Would you please pour the libations, Art?"

"Coming right up, sir!' Arthur popped the champagne cork.

Laurence raised his champagne glass. "To friends!"

"Cheers!" all responded.

Laurence proceeded to describe the early morning conversation with his rogue friend, Oliver Yates. "So it appears"—he concluded after ten minutes—"that my nightmare is about to end."

"I'm afraid not," Leopold said. "What you report is the worst possible news I could have imagined! Listen to me, Laurence. The Austrian domestic intelligence agency—the General Directorate for Public Safety— has been monitoring Franz Beitzel's actions for the past two years because of his contacts with *Ein Volk*, a Neo-Nazi group. Just yesterday, their surveillance of his cellphone picked up a conversation between Beitzel and—hold your breath, now!— Count von Strasser."

*"How's that possible?"* Laurence exclaimed.

"It's stranger than you can imagine," Leopold continued. "Federal agents followed Beitzel to der Demel yesterday morning, where he met with Oliver Yates!"

Laurence was on his feet, aimlessly pacing the room.

"Hold on! There's more," Leopold cautioned. "After leaving Yates at the café, Beitzel phoned von Strasser on his way back to his office. In that 30-second phone call, Beitzel revealed that he had information about their project—and would learn more about it later that evening."

"So now you're telling me that this 'friend'—who Oliver told me was going to solve the problem—is a goddamned Nazi?"

"To make matters even worse, it appears that he and Beitzel are meeting in Vienna *tonight*—in Oliver's hotel room."

"Well, then," Arthur interjected, "we're fucked!"

"It's a good thing you became an attorney instead of a detective," Leopold replied, "because ulcers would have killed you by now!"

Laurence had stopped pacing. "After all you've told us, Leopold, is there *anything* that can be done to stop this disaster from occurring?"

Leopold smiled. "They've placed the hotel under 24-hour surveillance. Nothing's going to happen to him. The question is: Will Mr. Yates turn over the Mozart fragment to Beitzel—believing he has completed his mission? If so, the agents will apprehend Beitzel and recover the fragment. Our story will have a superbly happy ending!"

Linn, who until now had been only a spectator, spoke up. "But what if Yates doesn't give him the fragment?"

"Why the hell wouldn't he?" Arthur asked.

"Well," she continued, "What if Yates has second thoughts about the matter? He's seriously concerned about the way Laurence regards him at this point. Suppose, having spoken to Laurence this morning, and having created this mess in the first place, Yates decides to return it *to Laurence* after all?"

Laurence nodded. "Oliver and I go back a hell of a long time. He's always been a loyal, dependable friend. We've been through a lot of shit together. I know he's suffering conflicting emotions right now, and yes, Linn, your scenario sounds plausible. We'll just have to wait and see how this cluster fuck turns out."

Leopold got up, walked to the fireplace. "Linn, if Mr. Yates manages to escape the Nazis *and* give the special agents the slip—that would indeed be some kind of Mission Impossible. But our guy, *Oliver* Cruise has managed to get *this* far, how can we write him off? So, you're right, Laurence. Only time will tell—and it won't be a long time."

# Chapter 18

The first concert of Christopher's inaugural recital tour, in Paris, had been a resounding success. *Now I've got even more practice hours to put in before moving on to Amsterdam. But first, I'm going to jog around town and warm up.*

While Christopher jogged along the narrow streets of the Left Bank and through the campus of Sorbonne University, Jeff and Margie were writing postcards to friends back home and planning shopping and dining excursions for their final day in the French capital.

"Why don't we take Christopher to that spectacular place on the Champs Elysees tonight?" Margie suggested. "You know, the one on the second floor overlooking the boulevard. Remember that elegant red damask wallcovering—and those posh crystal chandeliers? *Laduree*, that's the place! He loved that ritzy dining room, especially those exotic French pastries!"

"Sure, let's go there," Jeff said. "What the hell's another thousand Euros or so? CJ's earned it."

"And I'm treating *you* to lunch today at that superb restaurant in the Musee d'Orsay," Margie said.

"Well, you won't get any argument from me on that one, either, honey." Jeff hugged her. "And I'll have the best looking blond in Paris on my arm! So let's head for it right now."

When Christopher returned to the hotel, he showered and dressed, then devoured a ham-and-brie baguette sandwich, washing it down with a glass of Perrier water. Minutes later he was sitting at the upright piano in their suite, opening the score for the Mozart

Piano Sonata he would be performing in Amsterdam. *An Allegro Maestoso—just as dynamic as I am feeling right now!*

After finishing the first movement, he sat back. Margie and Jeff appeared in the room.

"I can't wait to hear you wow them with that in Amsterdam," Margie said. "Dad and I are leaving now, but I wanted you to know that we've made a reservation at Laduree for tonight. So, get your taste buds flowing!" She kissed Christopher on the cheek.

"Fantastic, mom!"

"See you later, CJ!"

Christopher ended the passionate second movement with a flourish and a sense of liberation. He pumped his fist in the air. "I'm ready for you, Amsterdam!"

# Chapter 19

After his call to Laurence Kellerman, Oliver Yates resumed his walk along the Kohlmarkt on a pleasant late spring day in Vienna. Residents and tourists packed the trendy shops, and tables were at a premium at the cafes and restaurants along the fashionable shopping promenade. The early tourist season had already begun. Oliver scanned the celebratory crowds, remembering his previous visits there. He and his late wife, Amelia, had enjoyed their honeymoon in the city, and it was in the same month of May that he attended his first international training conference there as a special agent. He took a deep breath of the fresh spring air, relieved that he would soon resolve the debacle he himself had created. A buzzing ended his daydream. "Hello!"

"I'm bloody damned glad I nicked you, Yates. Listen, you've got to get out of Vienna. You're in serious trouble, mate!"

"Corbyn? What in all of heaven are you jabbering about?"

"That bloke you met with earlier! He's deeply involved in a Neo-Nazi cabal that Austrian Intelligence has been tracking. They must be quite curious, indeed, about the sudden involvement of a British intelligence officer in their clandestine plot. You've got to leave right away!"

"Beitzel a Neo-Nazi?" Oliver struggled to believe such a revelation. "And what do you mean by 'right away'? I'm walking along the Kohlmarkt, and I'm not even close to my hotel. It's on the other side of the city, so I can't just—"

"You can't go back to that bloody hotel *at all*, mate! Get your ass on a train back to London as quickly as possible. Otherwise you're going to find yourself in real trouble."

"But I—"

"No buts about it, chum. Get to the bloody station now and evacuate the city! They've certainly staked out your hotel by now. Grab the soonest train to London you can get. I'll catch up with you once you've returned."

"Hold on to your knickers, mate. I understand what you're saying. I'm just trying to get my bearings on this wanked-out scene. Okay?"

"Of course, Oliver. But *please*, just call me when you've finally parked your arse on a train. Get going, man!"

"Consider me already gone!"

The time on his cellphone read 17:08 when Oliver Googled the app for the next train to London: "17:36 from the Hauptbahnhof," he read on the screen. "I can make it!"

He raced to the end of Kohlmarkt and hailed a taxi at Michaelerplatz. Within minutes he was speeding along Reitschulgasse. Ten minutes later the cab turned off Augustinstrasse and entered the drop-off area in front of the modern glass structure housing Vienna's central transportation center.

Oliver stuffed a bunch of Euros into the driver's hand as he exited the back seat. Entering the massive station, he spotted the *Fahrkarten* window and hustled to the ticket booth in front of it. The huge digital clock across the way read 17:23. *Plenty of time!* But an elderly man—the only person ahead of him— was having trouble understanding the ticket agent's instructions. By the time the old man finally shuffled away, the clock read 17:30.

"One first class to London on the 17:36, please," Oliver blurted out.

"That'll be 375 Euros, sir."

Oliver reached into his wallet and handed the clerk 400 hundred Euros.

"Thank you, sir, but I'm not sure you can get to that track on time," the agent said, glancing at the red digits blinking on the huge board across the concourse.

"I'll get there!" Oliver said, snatching the ticket and dashing for Track B49.

"All aboard!" the conductor yelled as Oliver neared the train. It was already departing when he got there. Jamming his right arm into the edge of the closing door, he forced himself inside. The door shimmied shut. Oliver Yates was on his way to London. Sinking into his seat, he reached into his coat and felt for the lower pocket. His fingers traced the edges of the small envelope containing Mozart's last words in their acrylic-protected sleeve.

It had been Oliver's plan to hand the fragment over to Franz Beitzel when they met that morning so he could ensure its safe return to the Austrian National Library—its ultimate reunification with the autograph manuscript. When Franz reacted in an unexpectedly frantic way, Oliver changed his plan, deciding to wait until later that evening when they could discuss the matter in a calm and more thorough manner. He needed to be certain he was taking the right action.

Alone in the first-class car, Oliver soon noticed the conductor approaching.

"Are you quite all right, sir? You nearly had your right arm severed back there." A smile had replaced the conductor's earlier frazzled expression of concern at seeing Oliver's risky entry.

"Quite all right, thank you. I apologize for my death-defying feat, but I've got to get back to London as soon as humanly possible."

The conductor tilted his black cap back a bit. "She must be well worth the risk!" he remarked as he moved on to the next car.

Oliver pulled out his phone and punched in Corbyn's number. His call went directly to voicemail. "Oliver here, David. I just nicked the 17:36 out of Vienna. I've got to change trains in Frankfurt and Paris, but I expect to be back in London around six tomorrow afternoon. I'll call you when I get in. I owe you one, mate."

When Franz Beitzel arrived at the pension hotel just before seven o'clock that evening, three Austrian intelligence officers, who had been there for several hours, had already searched Oliver Yates's room, finding nothing other than an overnight bag and some personal-care products.

"Mr. Beitzel, I've just checked Mr. Yates's room, as you requested, and he's certainly not there. You may want to call him again. You know how popular the Kohlmarkt can be! He may be lingering at a café there on such a gorgeous evening."

"There must be some mistake, Mr. Froede!" Franz was leaning on the small front desk as he spoke. "Mr. Yates is expecting me. We've got an appointment. It doesn't make any sense. It's so damned strange!"

"These are strange times, Mr. Beitzel," the manager said, just as the library director turned and bolted away.

The intelligence officers remained outside the hotel until midnight, and when Yates did not return to the hotel, there was no reason for them to continue their plan to apprehend Yates and Beitzel for questioning. Two of them departed, leaving only one officer to watch the hotel.

When further investigation showed that Oliver Yates had been a longtime friend of Franz Beitzel—predating the assistant director general's involvement with *Ein Volk*—and that Oliver was on holiday, they concluded that the meeting between the two friends earlier that day at the café had been merely coincidental. The case of Oliver's potential participation in the Neo-Nazis' scheme was dismissed.

"Yates is gone! I just got back from his hotel—*he's not there.*"

"What's happening up there, Beitzel? I thought you had this screwed-up mess under control. How could he be *gone*?"

Franz Beitzel hesitated. He had witnessed the count's anger once before—and it hadn't turned out well for the agent who had upset the Neo-Nazi boss.

"I've just hacked into his cell. He might've caught the 17:36 train to London."

"Well, what now? What do you expect me to do, pull off another Great Train Robbery?"

Franz wracked his brain for a solution.

"The train makes stops in Frankfurt and Paris. Can you send someone up there to get onboard? Maybe you could—"

"How many goddamned chores have you lined up for me today, you fool? I'm already exhausted by your incompetence."

The last thing Beitzel ever wanted to hear was the sound of the count's goons knocking on his door during the middle of the night.

"It's just a thought, sir. If we—if you— could get someone onboard that train you could get to Yates and find out what he knows about the artifact. It seems like—"

"Beitzel, do you want to put all this down in an instructional memo and send it to me? How fucking stupid do you think I am? Of course that's what *we* will do! I'll dispatch someone to Frankfurt right away. Just sit tight in case—for some unfathomable reason—I might need you."

# Chapter 20

Outside Laurence's apartment, Linn, Leopold, and Arthur awaited the elevator.

"You said earlier that you had a follow-up at the doctor's today," Arthur said, turning to Leopold. "How'd it go?"

"My brain's about to explode. She says I've got an aneurysm or some such thing. What next!"

"Come on, dad. Dr. Ricker's diagnosis wasn't so bleak," Linn said. "It's a tiny growth. We'll have to see what the MRI results show before we know what to do. Try to be positive about it."

Linn turned to Art as the elevator door opened. "I need to ask you a big favor, Art. Dad's gonna need some tests and perhaps a few treatments to nip his condition in the bud. I'd like to go back to Brussels with him to get his appointments set up. And remain with him until everything's completed."

"Of course, Linn, anything I can do to help. Take all the time you need to get things sorted out." He nudged Leopold. "Make sure this old buddy of mine's in great shape."

Leopold was having none of it.

"You folks are up to your eyeballs in international intrigue, and you want me to take one of your best resources—*the* best—away from you now and turn her into a nurse? Hell no!"

Arthur looked straight into the old detective's eyes. "But you'll be getting the best care possible. I want your daughter to be there with you. There's nothing Linn can do here. It's all in the hands of the police."

"Well, this has been one hell of a vacation! First, I step into a Neo-Nazi plot, then I find my brain's about to explode. And now I'm supposed to abscond with the top strategist in your organization!"

"Really, Leopold, we're gonna be just fine," Arthur insisted, dodging Leopold's all-too-familiar dramatic routine.

"It's settled, dad. I'll make the reservations when we get back home. So just relax, okay?"

"What else can an old retired cop do? I'm outwitted by two of the best legal minds in Manhattan."

Linn reserved her ticket for the flight that Leopold had arranged for his trip back to Brussels, but she changed his from coach to first-class in the seat next to hers. *Wait 'til he finds out about that! I'm gonna get a lecture about my liberal spending habits.*

"All done, dad, I've gotten a ticket on the flight you had booked. We'll be leaving the day after tomorrow."

"You're spoiling the old man."

"But he's so eminently spoilable!"

# Chapter 21

Sergeant Lukas Rieger was off on another of Count von Strasser's do-or-die missions. Unlike the last job in Vienna, however, when he had to drive all night from Salzburg to Laurence Kellerman's hotel, for this assignment in Frankfurt he had the luxury of flying. Rieger checked his flight reservation, then the attached train ticket from Frankfurt to Paris. He pulled up the photograph of Oliver Yates attached to the count's email that morning.

"Why the hell do I always get stuck hounding such oddballs like this?" he mumbled. "Why don't I ever get some gorgeous *fraulein* to track down, and—" A buzz interrupted his complaint. "Yes, count, yes, yes, I got the photo—I'm leaving for the airport right now and—"

"Stop, Rieger! We've got eyes on Yates. We've confirmed that he's onboard the Frankfurt-to-Paris train—in the first car. He is going all the way to London. You copy that?"

"Got it, count. What's the move?"

"You've got to detain Yates before the train leaves Paris for London. Beitzel now thinks our man may have the fragment with him. You need to get him to a place where you can search him and retrieve it."

"Copy that, count."

"We've reserved your flight back to Salzburg from Paris at 16:35. That should give you plenty of time to get your hands on the object— or at least find out what the old Brit *knows* about it. Understand?"

"Check, check, and check!"

"What! No questions, Rieger? Are you sure you're straight with this?"

"Straight as I can possibly be."

"Okay, get back to me as soon as you've got results."

Then Rieger did have a question. "So, uh, what about the Brit? I mean what the hell am I supposed to do with him after I've got what we want?"

"Rieger, you've been around this game a long time! You know you can't allow anyone who's able to identify you to put *you*—or *our cause*—in a compromising position." The count's impatience punctuated the answer.

"And I've got to get all of this done in time to make the 16:35 flight?"

"Rieger, you've got the whole damned day!"

"Yeah, well, in that case, I won't waste a second, sir."

"*Wiedersehen.*"

"Goodbye, count."

※

Oliver Yates rested his head on the back of the leather seat as he waited for the train to leave from Frankfurt for Paris. *Ah, four and a half hours to unwind.* He had barely settled himself when his phone buzzed.

"Yates, old man, it's Corbyn. You've been *made*! Interpol has intercepted phone conversations between von Strasser and a 'Sergeant Rieger.' They believe he's the same wank that followed me to the airport in Vienna. Anyway, they're coming for you, Oliver. Their man will board your train right there in Frankfurt."

Oliver bolted upward in his seat. "David, the bloody train's about to pull out of the station," he whispered into the phone. "The bastard's probably on board already."

"Then get the hell off that train *now*, old chum, even if you've got to set off the emergency alarm. Someone's on the way to the station's main entrance to extract you. Look for a black Range Rover."

"Got it. I'm out of here, mate!"

Oliver bounded toward the exit at the rear of the car, bowling over a burly, well-dressed man pushing his way forward to the front.

Oliver got to the door as it was closing. He lunged forward, barely managing to roll out onto the platform as the train pulled away. The same conductor who had witnessed Oliver's entry antics on the trip from Vienna witnessed the scene replayed in reverse. "It's time I retired from all this nonsense once and for all," he muttered, as much bemused as bewildered.

Brushing off his coat as he got up from the aisle, Rieger winced in pain, grasping his shoulder that had slammed against the arm of one of the seats.

Back inside the station, Oliver was still catching his breath as he watched the train to Paris departing. He made his way through the crowded station toward the main entrance—bumping, apologizing, nodding, tripping—finally reaching the outside. Seeing no sign of a black Range Rover, he panicked. Shielding his eyes from the blinding late afternoon sun, he strained to identify vehicles farther away from the entrance. *No black Range Rover! No Rover of any color!*

Lukas Rieger collapsed into his seat as the train whisked him off to Paris. He yanked out his phone and called Count von Strasser.

"What is it, Rieger? Have you got him?"

"Count, uh, I think it was Yates who knocked me over just after I boarded the train and was heading down the aisle of the first car. I'm sure he jumped off—it must have been close! By the time I was back on my feet, the train had already pulled away from the station."

There was no response. Count von Strasser had disconnected the call and was punching in the phone number of his Frankfurt contact.

"The fucking moron bungled it as I feared! Yates expects to be picked up in front of the Hauptbahnhof in a black Range Rover. He's wearing a dark blue sport coat with grey flannel trousers. I've attached his photo. You need to intercept him before the Federal Police get to him first. Can you get him?"

Anton Sonntag had experienced von Strasser's wrath only once, but it was enough to know that he could not risk experiencing it again.

"I got this, count. Menges and I will nab him."

"Get back to me as soon as you've got him."

※

Still seeing no sign of a Rover, Yates reached for his cellphone. Before he even finished entering David Corbyn's number, a shiny black van screeched to a halt in front of him, the driver-side back door swinging open. Oliver jumped in. "Bloody hell! You fellas really like seeing a bloke sweat it out!" he said, collapsing onto the back seat, relieved at last.

The only response he heard was the sound of door locks bolting shut. He scanned the vehicle. *This isn't a Range Rover!*

"What's going on," he yelled as the black Mercedes-Benz GLC sped out of the station, onto the boulevard leading out of the city. "Stop! Why are we leaving Frankfurt? We're supposed to be—"

"Stay calm, Mr. Yates," a voice with a distinct German accent responded, "and there won't be any problem. We've got a long drive ahead of us, so just sit back and relax."

"What's happening? Who *are* you wanks? You're certainly not Brits!"

"We have no further information for you, Mr. Yates. When we get to Salzburg, you'll get all the answers you need," the voice responded.

"And maybe more questions," another voice added, laughing as he spoke.

"Salzburg! Why are you taking me there?"

His kidnappers did not respond.

The sun had nearly set as they headed south. A cold evening breeze from the slightly opened front windows chilled the back seat.

Sonntag was boasting on his cellphone. "Menges and I've got him, count! We're on our way back." Oliver Yates slumped over. He was anything but calm.

※

Back at the Frankfurt Train Station, one of the agents assigned to rescue Oliver Yates had just thrown a tire iron into the trunk of their Range Rover when the phone inside the vehicle buzzed.

"What in blazes are you fellas doing out there?" a voice from their command center demanded. "I've just been told they've taken Yates!"

"A flat tire shut us down on our way to the station," Agent Daniel Kemble yelled into the phone.

"Kemble, the GPS locator on Oliver's cellphone has enabled Interpol to continue tracking him," the command center said. "They're leaving the city and heading south in a black Mercedes. We'll get reinforcements out there to intercept them—but get your ass onto Highway 3 and drive south as fast as you can!"

"We're on our way," Kemble replied, as the Range Rover patched out of the train station driveway.

※

Oliver slowly extracted his cellphone as his kidnappers rattled on about not having any dinner and their need for a couple of beers. Placing the phone low on the floor, he stretched forward, pressing the speed dial to Corbyn's number, turning up the volume for outgoing calls. When Corbyn's ID appeared on the screen, Oliver addressed his kidnappers. "Do you blokes mean to tell me we're going all the way to Salzburg for a couple of cheap beers! Why wait so damned long? Hell, that's more than six hours away."

Listening to the prattle on the other end of the line, Corbyn patched the call to the Interpol unit at the MI6 headquarters. "Corbyn here. Yates managed to activate his cellphone. They're taking him to Salzburg. I'll keep you patched in."

# Chapter 22

Christopher Lambert stretched his long legs and placed his size eleven stocking-clad feet onto the seat across from him, gazing out the window as the train left for Brussels. Margie was seated next to him, opposite her husband.

"I hate leaving this marvelous city, especially after that fantastic reception last night," Christopher moaned. "Julie would have loved this trip."

"Well, buddy, we're on the Thalys—the fastest train on earth," Jeff reminded him, "so we'll be arriving in the gin-and-chocolate capital of the world in less than two hours. Rest your weary body, son."

"You were just spectacular, CJ. They loved every note. I, too, wish Julie could have seen you perform," Margie said.

"Maybe next time," he mused, thinking about Julie—far away on the West Coast of the United States as he sped through Europe in the opposite direction. "Anyway, we've saved the toughest crowd 'til last. I know those Brussel sprouts are damned keen on classical music, and their critics are the toughest in Europe. So, I think the gin will have to wait until the day after the recital. But the chocolate? I'm gonna dive into that as soon as we get off this train."

Jeff shot a glance out the window. "Look at that spectacular canal—and those handsome, Flemish-style brick homes along the water's edge. What a marvelous place!"

"Goodbye, Amsterdam," Christopher mumbled. "If it's Tuesday, it must be Belgium ... not San Francisco!"

※

When they arrived in Brussels, Christopher and his parents walked through the expansive Central Station, emerging onto the plaza in front of the Hilton.

"What a fantastic location, Dad. How did you ever pick this hotel out?" Christopher asked, admiring the plaza and, in the distance, the Grand Place.

"Just wait until you hear the stories I've got to tell you about the time I spent here with your Uncle Ricky," Jeff replied. "There's a lot of surprises waiting for you, CJ."

After admiring the centuries-old stone buildings surrounding the hotel, Margie turned her attention to Jeff and Christopher. "I can't imagine what your father has in store for us, Chris. From what he's been telling me all these years, he and your uncle really made their mark on this city when they were last here more than two decades ago."

"Now let's not jump right into it, honey. We'll give CJ a little at a time." Jeff put his arm around Margie, escorting her to the hotel entrance.

Christopher stood in the center of the lobby, scanning the bright white marble columns and gleaming white tile floor, his eyes focusing on the crystal chandeliers overhead and up to the vaulted ceiling.

"Yeah, your old Uncle Ricky sure did know how to pick them," Jeff said as they approached the front desk.

"Lambert party," Jeff announced.

"Ah, certainly, sir, we have two adjoining rooms on the third floor, facing the old city as you requested. Have you stayed with us before, Mr. Lambert?"

"Before you were even born, son."

"Then it *has* been a long time, sir!" the greying middle-aged man retorted, handing them their keys.

"But we'll be back again before you retire—*I promise.*"

Jeff turned and began walking toward the elevators He stopped in the center of the lobby, overwhelmed by the memory of that evening long ago when, at that exact spot, he and Heinrich had met with Matt and Leo. *What a nightmare that festive night turned into!*

"Honey, are you okay?" Margie intruded.

"Oh, sorry. Yes, quite all right, dear. Let's head to our rooms so we can get CJ to the Grand Place for the cocktail hour!"

Christopher noticed his father's brief transformation. "It is going to be one hell of an end to this trip."

"Just wait until Matt and Leo arrive," Jeff said. "This place is gonna take on a totally new atmosphere. Who knows what the hell they've got up their sleeves!"

# Chapter 23

Leopold Beckers was sorting out his clothing and effects on his bed, preparing for their flight to Brussels, when he turned to his daughter. "You know, darling, I originally planned on using this trip to break away from the usual humdrum life I was leading at home," he remarked, "but, my God, I never imagined it would turn into a three-ring circus!"

Linn was stuffing a blouse into her suitcase. "Yeah, let's see: your aneurysm, Laurence's disappearance, and—in the center ring— Wolfgang Amadeus Mozart! ... I'll finish my packing in a minute, but first, I've got to contact Art. He had one final item to check on for me. We've got to get to Kennedy by two."

"Certainly, Linn, go right ahead. I've got a bit more to finish here."

Linn walked to her bedroom and phoned Art. "Just checking in. What's the latest?"

"You're not gonna believe it, Linn! Just when we thought they had a bead on Yates in Frankfurt, it turns out he's gone missing. Interpol is trying to track him down. Detective Cummings has been communicating with the FBI about Interpol's latest information."

"What's going to happen next, Art? Maybe when we get to Brussels dad can get more help from his colleagues and find out what's going on."

"This is really eating Laurence up. He's not able to concentrate on anything else right now. It's consuming him completely."

"I'm so damned sorry to leave you in a lurch like this. You really need my—"

"Your *dad* needs you right now, Linn. Stop worrying about me or anything around here. Get him the best treatment you can find, and let's hope it works. I love the guy, Linn."

For the first time in years, Linn felt a close connection with Arthur. He really did care about her dad.

"You and I have a lot to catch up on, Linn. Let's talk more when you return, okay?"

"I'd love that," she said, her voice brimming with a passion Arthur had never felt from her before.

"These guild houses are magnificent," Christopher observed, as he and his parents walked along the cobblestone plaza, its 17th-century stone Flemish facades dotting the perimeter of the square.

"It's great to see you relaxed, honey," Margie said. "You really need this break after all your globetrotting keyboard performances this week."

"I've got to make this afternoon and evening count big time. I'll be practicing all day tomorrow and part of Thursday. Then, it's on to the final gig before I can really let loose and party."

Jeff's thoughts drifted back twenty years to the time when he and Heinrich had partied at the high-end cafes and restaurants in the city. "Just try absorbing all of this, kids! This is the most magnificent town square in all of Europe. And wait until tonight when they light up the entire area—you're not gonna believe it."

They took seats at a small table on the edge of the square. Jeff summoned the waiter and they ordered cocktails, Margie leading the charge.

"How can I possibly resist a chocolate martini?" she said. "We *are* in Belgium!"

Jeff and Christopher each ordered White Rain gin on the rocks.

"To the calm before the storm!" Jeff toasted. "Matt and Leo arrive tomorrow morning. Who knows how soon things will start spinning out of control?"

By seven o'clock the next morning, Christopher had already left for the Flagey center. As he crossed the square and approached the grand Art Deco building, he paused before entering. *Some of today's greatest musicians performed here early in their careers—Yo-Yo Ma, Lang Lang ....*

Taking a deep breath, he entered the lobby. "Good morning, sir. I'm Christopher Lambert. I'll be performing tomorrow night, so—"

"Ah, yes, Mr. Lambert," a short, balding elderly man responded. "I'm Joseph, the head usher here." He checked the clipboard on his desk. "Yes, the piano has been set up for you in concert hall 4. Just walk to the end of the lobby and turn right. The entrance is located at the end of that corridor."

"Thank you, sir."

"Just call me 'Joseph,' young man," he said. "And please let me know if there's anything you may need."

"Thanks so much, Joseph," Christopher responded, turning toward the hall.

As he entered the concert hall, the simple elegance of the place dazzled him. Plush red seats lined the pristine pinewood floor, and the soft wooden balconies cantilevered on three walls created a warm, cozy atmosphere for the hall's nine hundred concertgoers. He turned to the stage. A gleaming black Baldwin grand piano beckoned to him from above the single step separating performer and audience. Christopher stepped onstage and placed his thin briefcase on the piano. He extracted sheet music and positioned it over the keyboard. He turned, walked to center stage, and bowed. When he had taken his seat at the piano, he struck the first note of Mozart's Sonata in A minor. Brilliant acoustics pulled the note forward, floating it to the third tier of the balcony, filling the young maestro with a confidence not felt in months.

# Chapter 24

On the train from Vienna to Frankfurt, Oliver Yates had slipped into the restroom, locked the door, and removed his jacket. Purchased at Harrod's shortly before leaving London on this new assignment, the handsome coat was his birthday gift to himself. He held the jacket in front of him, admiring the navy-blue Burberry, then removed a small white envelope from it, which he slipped into the back pocket of his trousers. Turning the jacket inside out, he draped it over the sink and, using his penknife, meticulously slit open a two-inch length of the hem at its bottom. *Ah, that should do it.*

Oliver pulled the envelope out of his pocket and opened it. He removed the acrylic sleeve and inserted it into the opening of the hem. Then he folded the end of the hem and fastened it with a small safety pin. Holding the jacket up again, he carefully examined it from the back. *Undetectable!* After another close inspection of the improbable, now sacred gabardine repository, he nodded his approval, and slipped the jacket back on.

Oliver Yates had removed his jacket and was pressing his back against the seat of the speeding Mercedes, holding the prized garment in his arms. Running his thumb and index finger repeatedly over the hem, he continued gazing wearily out the window toward the rapidly darkening horizon.

"Are you asleep back there, Mr. Yates?" Anton Sonntag's drill sergeant voice startled Oliver as his thoughts recounted the crushing day.

Oliver did not respond. There was still no sign of a rescue team. *Where in bloody hell are they?*

Darkness descended over the barren fields outside Wals-Siezenheim, four miles west of the center of Salzburg. Johann Menges yawned as he steered the Mercedes off Highway 8, entering A-1. Just then, a massive military-surplus Pinzgauer radio truck, blaring its gigantic blinding headlights, burst out of the shadows, ramming the right side of the Mercedes with such force that the black van became airborne. It landed twenty feet forward, tumbling over and plummeting down a steep embankment just north of the main runway of the Salzburg airport.

The violent collision slammed Oliver Yates against the left side of the Mercedes, smashing his head against the window and hurling him back across the seat, blood oozing out of his forehead. His cellphone flew out of his hand and jammed into the tracking under the front seat.

Four gypsies, each brandishing an AR-15 rifle, jumped out of the truck and surrounded the steaming wreckage of the Mercedes, which had come to rest against an immense rock at the bottom of the embankment. Forcing open the doors, they found the mangled corpses of Anton Sonntag and Johann Menges slumped over the front seat and floor. In the back seat was the lifeless body of Oliver Yates, embracing the last birthday gift he would ever receive.

While one stood guard, the other scavengers pushed their weapons aside and quickly began gathering their booty. Seeing the blue jacket in Oliver's death grip, one of the gypsies yanked Oliver's body away from the door and pried the jacket out of his arms. Spotting the Burberry label, he searched inside and removed the wallet, while another pulled off Oliver's cordovan shoes. Two of the other thieves followed the same routine in the front seats: scavenging the dead victims' firearms, clothing, rings, watches, cellphones. In less than ten minutes, the gypsies were back in the truck, speeding northeast out of the area, the signal from Oliver Yates's cellphone still jammed in the wrecked Mercedes—and pinging on the Interpol monitor.

"Look at this, everyone!" shouted Sergeant Janssens, at the Interpol headquarters in Brussels. "We had reason to believe they were headed for Salzburg. But this latest image"—Janssens had switched the cellphone tracking map to the mammoth monitor on the wall—"shows they've stopped suddenly at the outside perimeter of the airport. Get Corbyn back on the line!"

"Corbyn, here. What is it, sergeant?"

"Agent Corbyn, you've been following Yates's odyssey during the past few days. What do you make of this? The vehicle abruptly halted about fifteen minutes ago and hasn't moved since."

Corbyn was in silent panic, this sudden deviation presenting a scenario he feared to pursue.

"Corbyn, are you there? Corbyn?"

The veteran MI6 agent cleared his throat and exhaled. "Yes, yeah, I'm just trying to—"

"Listen, Corbyn! We've just received a report about recent activity in the area outside Wals-Siezenheim involving gang members of the gypsies and—"

"That's the worst-case scenario, Janssens. They're the most ruthless mob in the region. Those sons of bitches take no prisoners."

"We're in touch with the Austrian Federal Police," Janssens replied. "They've dispatched a team that should be arrive in about half an hour. I'll notify you as soon as we get an update from the field."

David Corbyn slumped in his chair. "Yeah, okay. Copy that."

Forty minutes later, after its fifth beep, Corbyn took a deep breath and finally pushed the answer button on his cellphone.

"Agent Corbyn, this is Rudolph Janssens. Sir, I have unfortunate news. We just got a report from the Austrian Federal Police that—"

Corbyn didn't hear the words that followed. His worst intuition about his best friend's fate had materialized. And Corbyn believed that he himself was responsible. Oblivious to the continued jabbering on the other end of the phone, he prayed as Janssens' voice faded: *We sipped martinis together for half a century. I'll savor every Tanqueray-induced moment of pleasure we shared, for the rest of my life. God speed, my dear Oliver. Can you ever forgive me? Is there—*

He interrupted himself long enough to ask, "Where are they taking him, Janssens?"

"He'll be moved to Landeskrankenhaus."

"I want to get him back here to London," Corbyn whispered. "He's got no one to manage all of this. I'll make sure he gets a proper burial … and settle all of his affairs. Will you let me know when I can arrange that?"

"Of course, David, I'll make certain that happens."

David Corbyn dropped his cellphone, and for the first time since his wife died, he wept.

By the time the Austrian police arrived at the demolished Mercedes, the gypsy gang had already traveled fifty miles northeast, stopping in Vorchdorf, where they junked the radio truck after unloading their day's worth of bounty into a dark green 2006 Citroen. By early the next morning, they had arrived at the outskirts of Vienna.

# Chapter 25

Linn Beckers and her dad arrived in Brussels, weary from the delayed flight and the emotional turmoil of the past two weeks. Opening the door to the home where she had grown up, Linn flicked on the lights, then froze. Everything appeared exactly the way she remembered it. For a moment she expected her mother to dash out of the kitchen and embrace her.

"Well, are we going inside, or have you decided to check us in at the Ritz Carlton instead?" Leopold chided.

"Sorry, dad. It's just that I haven't been back here since—"

"I know, honey. I often get the same feeling. Sometimes I expect your mother to greet me with a hug and kiss."

"Dad, you must get so lonely here. Can there be any pain worse than yearning for the one you love who is gone forever?"

"None," Leopold sighed, putting his arm around her.

"Sorry, dad. I didn't want us to start off like this. At least we've got each other to hug. ... Let me freshen up and fix us a drink and snack before bedtime."

"Now, that's my daughter talking!" Leopold closed the door and reached down for their luggage.

"Whoa, dad. Let me take those. It's time you got some rest."

"I hope you're not going to start treating me like a patient already. I can still carry a few bags a short distance without dropping dead."

"I just don't want you overdoing it. You don't know how heavy my luggage can be."

"It's a deal! You can take the heavy one."

Ten minutes later Linn entered the kitchen and, after a brief scavenger hunt through the kitchen cabinets, selected an unopened box of water crackers. She opened the fridge and removed a shiny blue and silver package of boursin cheese. *Still dad's favorite after all these years.* She placed the cheese in the center of a serving dish, arranging the crisp white crackers around the perimeter. A wine rack at the edge of the kitchen counter contained half a dozen bottles, from which she selected a Pinot Noir. Before Leopold returned, Linn had poured the light, fragrant wine and placed the glasses next to the cheese tray on the kitchen table. She sat down and scanned the room, remembering how proud her mother used to be when preparing her legendary dinners for family and friends. Imagining her mother humming as she tended to the pots and pans on the stove, Linn sipped the Pinot. *To you, mom!*

Leopold joined her at the table. "Ah! You continue to spoil me. Now that is exactly what I need right now. Welcome home, darling." Leopold took a sip of the wine. "Hmmm, a hint of cherries and blackberries."

"Excellent purchase, dad. A delicious aroma, too."

"Well, I must be honest, Linn. I don't know who gave it to me, but it was one of those thousands of gifts I received when I retired," he said, laughing at his own hyperbole.

"You were pretty damn popular for the old taskmaster image that brought you fame throughout Brussels. And, indeed, Belgium itself."

"Your flattery will get you everywhere! Listen, Linn, I can't tell you how much I appreciate all you've done for me, coming here when your office is struggling with such a catastrophe, looking after your ancient father's declining health."

"I can't imagine being anywhere else in the world right now, dad. We're going to get you through this episode and get you back on track. But I think we should start with a nice, jet-lag-conquering sleep and start fresh tomorrow—whenever we decide to get out of bed! One final toast before we collapse for the evening," Linn said. "To mom!"

"For all she's given me—especially you," Leopold replied.

※

116

Linn awoke at 10:30 the next morning. Before Leopold was out of bed she had showered and dressed and was preparing breakfast. The sourdough bread in the freezer would be the morning fare, enhanced by the raspberry jam and butter she found in the fridge. The strong, fragrant essence of the freshly brewed Lavazza summoned Leopold back to full consciousness and, within minutes, he was entering the kitchen.

"Mr. Van Winkle has finally awakened! Good morning, dad."

"If it hadn't been for the tantalizing aroma of that java, I might have slept until tomorrow. Good morning, honey."

"Dad, I've been clicking through my phone, checking the calendar of events in Brussels this week, and you're not going to believe who the Flagey is featuring tomorrow night. Remember when we attended the Mostly Mozart Festival that night, how completely caught up you were by the young pianist?"

"Sure I remember. It was the handsome young man whose initials, CJL, I've been trying to track down for the past twenty-five years. What about him?"

"That same young virtuoso is appearing tomorrow night at an event featuring up-and-coming musical artists at the Flagey Festival. So, I thought we could grab a nice dinner and check it out."

"I'd love to hear him perform again, and this time I'm going to meet him. I know the head usher at the Flagey, so I won't have any problem getting backstage afterwards." Leopold's thoughts drifted back twenty-five years to the tragedy at the Atomium.

"Is there anyone in Brussels you *don't* know?"

"Hah! Unfortunately, in my business you don't usually meet people in the best of circumstances. I met Joseph, the head usher, when a fascist mob mugged him at an anti-nuke rally back in the late seventies. I got him to hospital to treat a gash on his forehead. Anyway, four days later he showed up in the department with the biggest box of Godiva chocolates I have ever seen. After that sweet 'thank you,' we got together for coffee every now and then over the years. He worked at the Godiva plant most of his life and retired as a production manager. Joseph always loved music—all kinds—so volunteering for the Flagey was a natural."

"Then it's done! I'll reserve tickets for us. It will be a terrific way to ease into the medical appointment maze in which you're about to find yourself trapped."

Leopold finished his breakfast and got up from the table. "After I shower, I'll do some research in my old files in preparation for the big Flagey reunion tonight."

"I can hardly wait to see how this mystery unravels, Mr. Holmes."

"I may end up more astonished than you, my dear Watson."

# Chapter 26

When Christopher Lambert returned to the hotel after power walking for an hour around Brussels, he found a note on the fridge: *CJ, your dad and I have gone shopping. I've made a tuna salad sandwich for you and there's a bag of chips in the cabinet. Take a nap afterward. You must rest up for the big event tonight! Love, Mom*

He peeled the note off the fridge and opened the door. Sliding out the four-inch-high sandwich, he shook his head. *That is one hell of a snack!* He was finished in just fifteen minutes. He shaved and showered, and was soon back in the bedroom, scanning the music sheets in preparation for the concert. *In just six more hours, I'll be onstage,* he mused, glancing at the clock on the nightstand.

Two hour later, having completed his review, Christopher removed his tuxedo from the closet, hung it on the door, and checked it over one last time. He stepped over to the dresser and opened the bottom drawer, reaching to the back and pulling out a folded T-shirt; unravelling it revealed the slim, brown leather pouch containing the pewter cigarette case. "Couldn't possibly leave home without it!" he whispered, as he slid the pouch into the front right pocket of his tuxedo jacket.

Christopher's parents returned at four o'clock, loaded down with packages from every chocolate shop in the city. Jeff reached into one of the bags and popped open a small, red-and-gold ornately designed box of Cote d'Or chocolates bursting with hazelnuts, immediately stuffing two of the dark squares into his mouth. "Yo, you gotta try some of this Belgian magic," he called out to Christopher. "It'll certainly sharpen your performance tonight." Jeff popped another square into his mouth.

Arriving from his bedroom, Christopher chuckled at seeing the chocolate-induced exuberance running down from the corners of his father's mouth. "That chocolate smells damned good, dad," he said, taking two pieces out of the box. "Mom, are you going to join us? We'll open another box."

"You don't want to know how many of those Belgian temptations I've already given into today, dear," she replied. "I'm way over my normal sugar intake for the month."

"Want this last piece, CJ?"

"Nah, go ahead, dad. You enjoy it. I'm saving myself for those spectacular waffles with that Neuhaus chocolate syrup at the Galeries after dinner tonight. I'll be washing it all down with a mug of that incomparable Bouchard hot chocolate."

"You fellas just go ahead and devour those perishable delicacies while I examine these magnificent blouses I discovered in those little boutiques three blocks from here," Margie interjected. "And what have you been doing all day, CJ?" she asked, holding up a blue silk blouse, inspecting it carefully as she spoke.

"I've read the reviews of the festival in this morning's paper. There's an awful lot of talent here. They were ecstatic about the violinist from Japan who wowed the audience yesterday afternoon. And you should read their praise of the tenor from Paris—incredible!"

"Now, listen CJ, I know that voice of yours," Jeff said, sated from his afternoon bonbon feast. "Don't be getting all verklempt about tonight. I hope those reviewers saved some of their classical bigshot verbiage, because they're gonna have one hell of a challenge describing your performance, son!"

Christopher laughed. "No, it's not that. I'm just amazed at the talent this festival attracts every year. It boggles my mind that I'm part of it all."

"Well, hell, *they're* the ones who should be thrilled!" Jeff countered. "After all, they were able to procure your already legendary talent."

Margie glanced at the clock.

"What time did you want us to leave for the concert hall, CJ? It's already 4:30."

"We should head over there in about an hour," said Christopher.

"Then I better get ready right now." She pointed at Jeff and Christopher. "You, too, guys. Let's get going."

※

"This is your dressing room, Mr. Lambert. You can put all your things in here," said the elderly gentleman who had directed Christopher to the concert hall the day before. There's also a pot of fresh coffee, sir."

"Wait a minute, Joseph," said Jeff.

"Is there something wrong, sir?"

"There's no star on CJ's dressing room door," Jeff chided, forming one with his hands on the center of the door.

Joseph nodded. "Correct, sir, the star is awarded *after* the performance."

"Ha! You got me on that one, pal!" Jeff replied.

As Joseph turned to leave, Jeff pressed a twenty-dollar bill into his palm. "Thanks for taking such diligent care of my son."

"I know he's going to be a big hit tonight," Joseph responded. "I heard him practicing yesterday—I'm already a fan!"

"You're far too kind, Joseph," said Christopher, placing the clothing bag holding his tuxedo on the hook on the closet door.

"Some coffee?" he asked.

"No, we better leave you alone so you can get ready," Margie said.

"You're gonna make Mr. Mozart real proud tonight, son," Jeff added on their way out.

※

Christopher was gazing into the mirror, putting on his black silk bowtie when he heard a knock on the door.

"Come in," he said, taking a last, hurried peek in the mirror.

Jeff and Margie were chatting as they entered.

"Wait until you see that crowd out there, CJ. I think you've got a full house."

Margie was straightening her son's tie. "Such a virtuoso you've become!"

"Just like his old man," Jeff laughed, patting Christopher on the back.

An usher tapped on the dressing room door. "Five minutes, Mr. Lambert!"

"Go get 'em, son!"

"It's all for you guys tonight," Christopher said as his parents left the dressing room.

While the festival director was introducing him, Christopher watched from backstage, surveying the sold-out crowd. He reached into the right-hand pocket of his jacket, squeezing the brown leather pouch inside. *I'm ready, Uncle Ricky.*

The festival director beckoned to Christopher to join him on stage. Enthusiastic applause greeted him. Christopher shook the director's hand, turned to the audience, and bowed twice After the second bow, he walked to the gleaming black Baldwin. As he sat before the piano, Christopher froze. All the practice, planning and drama before the concert seemed in vain. Staring at the black and white keys, he closed his eyes. *What am I supposed to be playing first?*

His memory had gone totally blank. Christopher pressed his sweating palms against his face, brushed back his hair, and closed his eyes. The audience stirred. A soft murmuring broke the silent anticipation in the concert hall. He reached inside his jacket pocket, and gently squeezed the pewter cigarette case. Within seconds all became clear to him. He raised his hands majestically over the keyboard, and plunged them with force onto the keys, instantly translating the pulsing chords of Mozart's Piano Sonata in A Minor, translating the great composer's theme of the dynamic passage from grief to resignation. The final forceful outburst of the first movement, like a storm breaking out in the concert hall, drew gasps from the audience.

Christopher raised his eyes toward the vaulted ceiling and began conveying the restrained passion of the second movement with its subtle air of dignity, concluding with a feeling of anguished passion that transfixed the audience. Growing more dramatic, he established a tragic mood, then, the Presto—his face now just inches from the piano keys. His entire persona coaxing soft, mellow notes out of the grand classic instrument, Christopher brought home the spectacular fluctuations, ending with a demonic, magical expression as, once again, he raised his hands high over his head, his hair tossing wildly in the air.

Impassioned applause erupted. The audience rose in unison as Christopher got up from the piano bench and strode to the edge of the stage. He bowed, hand over his heart, and waved to the crowd. His uncles were especially animated, as if cheering an Eagles game-winning touchdown.

Three rows behind Christopher's family, Leopold and Linn stood applauding. The sonata's tragic air and sense of final loss had invoked in Leopold thoughts of his wife, who had so much enjoyed attending concerts with him in that very hall.

Christopher returned to the piano to sustained applause, rewarding his new fans with Mozart's Piano Sonata in B flat major. Communicating the composer's delicate charm with a clear, transparent sound, he quickly brought a sense of calm back to the concert hall. The gentle flow of the second movement continued the tender melody. But then, following a hint of melancholy, Christopher finished with a loud, dramatic chord, delivering a witty, playful conclusion.

The cheering audience moved Christopher. He brushed away a tear as he bowed, holding his head down for fifteen seconds. Waving to the audience, he blew kisses repeatedly as he moved slowly offstage, savoring the adulation.

Jeff and Margie were already in the aisle as Christopher disappeared backstage. Matt and Leo squeezed their way apologetically through the crowd, following Christopher's parents. Not far behind, Joseph beckoned to Leopold and Linn, escorting them toward the dressing room. Christopher was sitting silently at the dressing room table, staring into the mirror, as his parents entered. Jeff approached and began massaging his exhausted son's shoulders. "Wolfgang, you sure took everyone for one hell of a ride tonight!" Margie took a seat next to her son. "You were incredibly amazing!" she said. "You totally owned them out there."

Mellowed by his dad's continuing deep massage, Christopher leaned back and sighed. "What a terrific audience ...."

Pushing open the dressing room door, Leo and Matt rushed in.

"Christopher-freakin'-Jeffrey-rockstar Lambert!" Matt greeted him with open arms. "Freddie Mercury would have given all his teeth for that kind of audience reaction!"

What a magnificent performance!" Leo chimed in.

"Thanks for being here, guys, and for those two massive urns of red carnations—what an incredible sight!" Christopher replied as he freed himself from his father's clutches.

Matt plucked one of the flowers off the arrangement. "This is all you need to complete that gorgeous tailor-made outfit of yours," he chuckled, carefully placing the carnation into the lapel.

Leo finally raised the unasked question: "What on earth was that nerve-wracking pause at the beginning of the concert all about?"

Christopher stood up and faced everyone. "You're probably not gonna believe this ... but when I sat down at the piano my mind totally blanked out. For a moment, I didn't even remember what I was supposed to be playing. I was terrified. So, I reached into my pocket and squeezed my lucky charm."

Gaping mouths all around him greeted this revelation, the silence interrupted only by Joseph swinging open the dressing room door and ushering in Leopold and Linn. Oblivious to their entrance, Christopher continued his explanation.

"For the past five years, since my first solo performance at Curtis, I've been carrying this souvenir with me for good luck. Christopher pulled the brown leather pouch out of his pocket and extracted the pewter cigarette case, holding it forth for all to see.

Jeff's eyes bulged. Uttering words at first impossible to understand, he finally screamed, "Where the hell did you *get* that, CJ?" His face crimson and eyes tearing, he demanded—even louder, *"Where did you get it?"*

At the back of the assembled group, Leopold's eyes had widened, as well. *Is this merely a coincidence?* he wondered. Arthur had recently told Leopold that someone had delivered the missing Mozart fragment to Laurence Kellerman in a pewter cigarette case inside a brown leather pouch, the description identical to what his eyes were now fixed on.

Christopher recoiled. Never having seen his father so angry, he feared him for the first time in his life. Holding the cigarette case in his left hand, he thrust out his right arm. "Hold on, dad! Let me explain." He handed the case to him. "You know that I always played in Uncle Ricky's den when I was a kid. Well, one day I was rifling through his bookcase when, Voila! I found this pouch behind a bunch of Mozart record albums."

"What's wrong, Jeff?" his wife asked. "Why is this upsetting you so much?"

Perspiring heavily now, but taking a deep breath, Jeff relented. "Sorry, everybody, it's just that I haven't seen this relic in more than twenty-five years. I'm stunned. That's all. I apologize for my insane outburst. Let's party!"

"We're all going to Le Marmiton for a spectacular celebration," Matt announced. Holding up his cellphone for all to see, he added: "And our table is ready right now. Let's get out there and celebrate!"

Christopher was only now noticing Joseph and the two strangers in the room. He went directly to them. "I'm so sorry, folks. With all this craziness, I didn't see you come in."

"No apology needed, Mr. Lambert. I'm sorry for intruding, but I want to introduce you to Leopold Beckers and his daughter, Linn, two of my best friends from Brussels. They asked if they could meet you."

"Thanks so much, Joseph. Good evening, I'm Christopher Lambert."

"My dad and I adored your performance at the Mostly Mozart Festival when he visited New York recently," Linn said. "When we returned to Brussels yesterday, we were fortunate to see the ad for tonight's recital on the internet. We just had to come!"

"I'm honored that you would consider seeing me perform *twice* in just a few weeks. Thanks so much," Christopher replied.

As Linn chatted with Christopher about their recent visit to New York, Leopold eased his way toward Jeff.

"I'm Leopold Beckers, Mr. Lambert. It's a pleasure to meet you."

" 'Jeff' please."

"You must be truly fond of that young man over there, Jeff," Leopold replied.

"I can't tell you what he means to me and how he enriches my life every day."

Leopold searched for the right words to begin.

"This may sound strange, Jeff, but I found something many years ago that I think could … belong to you."

Jeff laughed. "How the hell could that be? We've never even met before."

"I recently retired from the Brussels Police Department. I found the object about twenty-five years ago, but I would prefer not to interrupt your celebration tonight. Could we possibly meet tomorrow to talk about it?"

Intrigued by the peculiar scenario, Jeff studied the detective for a moment. "Well … uh … we leave on Tuesday afternoon, so I guess we could get together tomorrow morning. How about joining me for coffee at our hotel—the Hilton Centre—say, around ten?"

"That would be fine, Jeff. I look forward to seeing you then. Goodnight!"

Leopold joined Linn and Christopher. "Congratulations, young man! It was a magnificent performance. Thanks so much for indulging us."

"My pleasure, sir. Thanks for stopping by."

Half an hour later, led by Matt and Leo, Christopher and his parents entered Les Galeries Royal Saint Hubert. Matt slowed down and, turning back to them, yelled, "Just about halfway down this gorgeous, enclosed shopping center and we'll be there."

Matt's enthusiasm was contagious.

Christopher, staring high above their heads at the massive glass canopy over the gallery, grew dizzy for a moment and stopped. "What a spectacular place!" he replied to his intrepid uncles, who were five yards ahead, waiting at the entrance.

"Ah, good evening, folks," the maître d' said, once all were inside. "Welcome to Le Marmiton."

"Thanks. It is great to be back," Matt responded. "We have a reservation for Stephenson."

"Welcome back, sir," the maître d' replied. "We have the table-for-five upstairs exactly as you requested, sir."

"Wonderful! Thanks so much." Matt was beaming.

They followed the head waiter upstairs to a round table in the front corner of the elegant Belgian restaurant overlooking the expansive Gallery below, its trendy shops glowing beneath the glass canopy. Jeff was silent as they settled into their seats, his mind assaulted by memories of that evening twenty-five years earlier when Heinrich Winterbottom suffered a heart attack brought on by his elevated hypertension and the sudden news of his best friend's death.

A waiter presented the menus. "Good evening, folks. My name is Bryce. It is my pleasure to serve you this evening."

"Bryce, so good to have you," Matt responded. "Could you please bring us a bottle of Dom Perignon?"

"Right away, sir."

Margie, who had been gazing at the shops below, turned to Matt. "I must say, Matt, you two always know exactly the best place to go for a celebration—no matter where we are!"

Matt was looking around the room, recalling the last time he and Leo dined there with Jeff and Ricky. "This place holds some very pleasant and, at the same time, a few stark memories. We last dined here with Ricky about twenty-five years ago. He sat in that very spot where you're sitting, Margie."

Margie leaned across the table, her eyes fixed on Matt. "Unbelievable, Matt! To think we are sitting around the very table where my dear brother once had dinner—utterly amazing!"

"*Once* had dinner?" Jeff laughed. "Your brother was one of the most frequent diners at this establishment—for more than three years! The entire staff revered this table as a kind of shrine. Can you imagine the gratuities Ricky showered on them during his tenure here?" Jeff's eyes appeared distant for a moment.

"Here we are, folks, Dom Perignon!"

The champagne poured, they all rose and toasted Christopher.

"To the next Lang Lang!" Matt proclaimed.

The turmoil of the day had exhausted Christopher. He rose from his chair and toasted everyone, lifting his fluted glass precariously high in the air. "To all of you! I love you more than anyone in the world." As all turned their attention to the menu—sumptuous in itself—Margie groaned. "Every time I go out for dinner with you fellas, I gotta take my dress to the tailor for alterations the next day. And from the looks of this array of delicious offerings, it appears that tonight will be no exception."

"Hey, we only live once, my dear, so enjoy it!" Matt said. "And besides, you're way too humble. Jeff's one hell of a lucky guy to have a looker like you!"

"Yeah, but I'm afraid that I'm cutting that one life short," she replied.

The table grew raucous. Even the usually celebratory Belgians craned their necks toward their table.

"I suggest we order a mélange of appetizers so we can taste *everything*!" Matt more than suggested.

"Great idea!" Jeff replied, all agreeing.

"Excellent!" the waiter said. "And for your entrees?"

Matt turned to Margie. "How about starting us off?"

"Well, I'm gonna have the filet of cod with the mousseline sauce and boiled potatoes."

The waiter addressed Jeff. "And you, sir?"

"Well, there's no way in hell I'm gonna miss that rabbit leg in beer and cherries! I enjoyed that marvelous concoction decades ago. I've never forgotten those flavors!"

Christopher ordered the tenderloin steak with green pepper and cream, flambéed with cognac.

"This menu is even greater than I remembered," Matt said. "Duck a l'Orange with ginger—sold!"

Leo ordered the same as Margie. "And another bottle of Dom Perignon, please."

As they savored the appetizers—Belgian cheese croquettes, carpaccio with truffle oil and parmesan shavings, the salmon tartare, mussels with garlic butter, and warm goat cheese in puff pastry— Matt recounted the dinner with Ricky years before. "It was supposed to have been a festive occasion. Jeff had been here in Brussels for— what? three years?—taking care of Margie's dad as he was receiving those treatments at the research center. So Leo and I decided to come to Brussels for a reunion of sorts. We—"

Jeff interrupted. "Are you really gonna go into all the gory details of that horrible evening?"

"Sorry Jeff, but I had to say how surprised I was that night when Ricky revealed he was a close friend of Riley Warner—the best friend that Leo and I have ever had in our lives. What an incredible coincidence! Then, it turned out that Ricky had no idea that Riley had died. I mean, it just came out casually in conversation, but it was so shocking to Ricky that he collapsed right here—right where we're all now sitting!" Matt pointed to the space between Margie and Jeff's chairs. "That's where he fell."

The table grew silent. Tears formed in Margie's eyes as she thought about her brother's premature death.

"You know, Matt, all this is terribly sad, but somehow being here now in this place that Ricky loved so much is exhilarating. I'm glad you brought us here, and thanks so much for sharing that story. It means a great deal to me. I know how well Jeff had taken care of my dad when they were here, and I'm sure it added years to his life. So, thank you—both of you—for all of this."

"I'm happy I was able to help him. Now, let's get back to celebrating CJ!" Jeff looked around the table. "Is he still here?"

Christopher was sipping his third glass of champagne. "The more stories I hear about Uncle Ricky, the more I regret never having met him. But you fellas fill out his portrait quite colorfully. Thanks for that!"

After dinner, as the festive group strolled around the gallery, Matt continued his antics. "You guys can't possibly leave Brussels without enjoying a Belgian waffle topped with melted Belgian chocolate and fresh whipped cream!"

Margie was having none of it.

"No way in hell I'm gonna gorge myself at this hour. Sorry, Matt."

"Well, come on, then. You can watch *us* eat it. You won't gain any weight that way!"

Jeff laughed. "That would be like Belgian waterboarding my dear wife. Stop it, Matt!"

"Okay, how about you two take a nice long stroll around the Gallery and us men will gorge ourselves senseless with chocolate?"

"That's a deal," Jeff replied. "We'll see you guys in half an hour."

They returned to the hotel just before midnight. Christopher, intoxicated by the champagne and the success of the evening, removed his jacket and tie, unbuttoned his shirt, pushed off his shoes and flopped onto his bed. "If this is Belgium," he murmured, "Julie must be in San Francisco...."

# Chapter 27

When Christopher awoke mid-morning, he rubbed his temples, groaning, and realized he was still in his tuxedo. Moaning deeper, he thrust his head into the pillow and was soon asleep again.

Meanwhile, Jeff had returned to his room after finishing his workout in the hotel health club. Shortly after, he was leaving for his meeting with Leopold. "See you in an hour or so, babe."

"Matt and Leo said they have a surprise for lunch today," Margie reminded him. "They'll be here around 12:30. More food, more calories, more pounds—why not? I give up!"

Jeff kissed her, patted her ample butt, and hurried downstairs. Entering the lobby, he saw Leopold Beckers chatting with the hotel manager in front of the concierge desk.

Catching a glimpse of Jeff, Leopold ended his conversation with the manager and walked over to him. "Good morning, Jeff!" Leopold extended his hand.

"Hi, Leopold! Do you know *everyone* in Brussels?"

"Maybe too many, my friend," Leopold replied. "I see you've survived the gargantuan celebration for your son last night."

"Yeah, I have, but I'm not sure about our young virtuoso. He hasn't surfaced yet. Let's get some coffee. My head is splitting."

"You look pretty much the way I felt after my retirement party," Leopold chuckled, "but you're a hell of a lot younger!"

"This morning, I don't feel so young," Jeff mumbled.

They sat in the restaurant, its shiny brass light fixtures gleaming above the white marble floor. Jeff signaled the waiter. "A pot of coffee, bud, as hot and as soon as possible, *please*! Oh, and I'll have a couple of your marvelous croissants. ... How about you, Leopold?"

Leopold sighed, "Um ... oh, what the hell, I'll have a cheese Danish."

A few minutes of small talk later, Jeff addressed the topic that Leopold raised the night before, averting his eyes from his new acquaintance as he spoke. "Well, I gotta tell you, Leopold, that when you approached me last night about having something of mine from twenty-five years ago, you got my head spinning. And if it weren't for the massive amount of bubbly I consumed, I would probably have been awake all night—instead of just a few hours." He took a gulp of his java, crossed his arms in front of him, then looked directly at Leopold, awaiting his response.

Leopold had already begun preparing his response. *The Atomium tragedy has been taunting me for two and a half decades. This could be the moment that solves the mystery.* Finally, he began speaking. "Around the time you say you were here in Brussels, Jeff, a tragic incident occurred at the Atomium—you know, that unique structure built for the '58 World Expo, with its huge steel spheres and—"

"Yeah, of course I know the building," Jeff interrupted, his body stiffening. "I mean, it's world famous. But, uh, how could that possibly have anything to do with me?" He looked up and locked eyes with Leopold. "Anyway, didn't you say you had something that might belong to me? What's that got to do with a 'tragedy'—or anything else?"

"Well, Jeff, probably nothing at all." Leopold's tone was casual. "But I want you to see the object I found there." He reached inside his jacket and pulled out a small yellow envelope. Moving his cup aside, he placed the envelope in the center of the table, untucked the flap, and tilted the envelope. Out slid a small penknife. The overhead light shone brightly upon its pearly handle, illuminating the brilliant rubies and gold initials—*CJL*—on the surface.

"What!" Jeff exclaimed. "How could you *possibly* have this? Where the fuck did you get it?"

Leopold remained calm. "There's no need to be frightened or apprehensive about this, Jeff. Hey, if it belongs to you, okay—no problem, no worry—end of story. I'm just wanting to return it to its rightful owner. Nothing else, my friend."

Mesmerized by its magnificent beauty, Jeff reached over and slowly lifted the knife—reverently, holding it up to his eyes. Then he kissed it. "This belonged to my grandfather. Those initials, *CJL*, are his— *Christopher Jeffrey Lambert.*"

"Ah, yes! That's what struck me first about this handsome knife. When I saw that name on the program on the evening my daughter and I attended your son's concert in New York, it suddenly registered with me."

" 'Christopher Jeffrey Lambert,' yes! I named my son for him. My grandfather was the most loving person in my life. I know you'll find this hard to believe, but when I was a kid, I entered a seminary to study for the Catholic priesthood."

Leopold maintained his silent interest as Jeff continued.

"My grandfather, you see, was an ultraconservative Catholic— an officer of the Knights of Malta. He always wore plain black clothing. When he heard that I was planning to become a priest, he was overjoyed. Do you know what he said to me, Leopold? He told me that I had made him happier than he had ever been in his whole life. I will never forget the look in his eyes—conveying the deepest feeling of love for me that I've ever received. It was at that moment he removed *this knife* from his pocket, presenting it to me as in a sacramental ritual—rewarding me for the joy I had brought him." Jeff's eyes remained fixed on the beloved heirloom.

Leopold was visibly moved, but he had to find out how that knife got to the Atomium in the first place. "He must have loved you very much, indeed, Jeff, but how could this exquisite gift have turned up in the Atomium of all places?" he said, studying Jeff's reaction.

Jeff was already back at the Atomium as Leopold spoke, reliving that terrifying night, just as in his unending nightmares. The shocking sight of his grandfather's knife unleashed feelings he had been suppressing for years.

"Leopold, I've never told a single, solitary person in the entire world about what happened there that night," Jeff began.

"You mean—the time the horrible tragedy occurred that I mentioned earlier?"

"Yes, yes, of course! My best friend, Heinrich, Margie's brother, had asked me to do a favor for him. He said that a colleague just discovered the location of a precious artifact that someone had stolen from him. The thief had hidden it under a step in one of those steep stairways inside the Atomium. He begged me to retrieve it for him."

Leopold imagined how priests must feel when hearing the lurid confessions of penitents as Jeff continued.

"When I got to the Atomium, I managed to get into the building by forcing open one of the doors in the back of that strange place. I immediately went to the exact location—sixth stairway, twenty-sixth step—just as Heinrich, with his usual precision, had described it. But whoever put the artifact under that step had used industrial-strength duct tape to fasten it. What made it even worse, workers had painted over it—God knows how many times over the years. So, I removed this very penknife from my pocket—I carried it with me all the time—and after a couple of minutes of scraping and cutting, I managed to release the object. In the process, however, the knife slipped out of my hand and fell to the floor. Anyway, the object I found was a pewter cigarette case. Yes, the same case that CJ, last night in the dressing room, elevated for all of us to see—like Moses displaying the Ten Commandments!"

"What a shock that must have been," Leopold sighed.

"Well—yeah! But 'shock' isn't the right word—*rage* is more like it."

"Of course, sure—after twenty-five years, I can imagine. When you were at the Atomium that night, did you ... uh ... see or hear anything odd—like maybe a gunshot or something?"

Jeff grabbed a croissant from his plate and bit off half of it, chewing the pastry voraciously. He pushed himself away from the table and, arms folded against his chest, laughed uncontrollably, crumbs falling from his lips. "Did I hear *a gunshot*? Ha! I was the fucking target! If it weren't for that precious cigarette case, I wouldn't be here today speaking with you—or, for that matter—with anyone. That's how the damned thing got dented."

"Was it a security guard that shot at you? Were you spotted by him or something?"

Jeff drained the remaining coffee in his cup, wiped his lips, then leaned across the table, his face just inches from Leopold's. "My friend, it was no cockamamie security guard. It was my totally fucked-up ex-brother-in-law, Larry Ingles."

Leopold instantly recognized the name from the files he had reviewed the night before.

"But, Jeff, why would he—"

"The poor guy had just returned home from Vietnam with a severe case of Post-Traumatic Stress Disorder. Somehow, he got it into his crazy noggin that I caused my ex-wife Barbara's sudden death while he was crawling around in those agent-orange-ravaged jungles. I mean, Barbara meant the world to him. She was all he had after their parents passed away. I don't know what pushed him over the edge, but he vowed to find me and kill me to get his goddamned delusional revenge. The sucker followed me all the way here to Brussels, where he at last tracked me down!"

Jeff was lying. Larry Ingles never suffered with Post-Traumatic Stress Disorder. He had served two years with the U.S. Army's Corps of Engineers in Vietnam, earning a Distinguished Flying Cross and a Bronze Star for meritorious service in combat. Larry and Barbara had enjoyed a close relationship during their childhood. When she told Larry about Jeff's infidelity, heavy drinking and physical abuse, Larry was furious.

Barbara divorced Jeff three months into their marriage after the night he grabbed her by the throat, strangling her until she passed out. Three days later, Barbara suffered a stroke while asleep—and died from cardiac arrest. When her doctor told Larry that strangulation had caused her death, Larry's reason for living changed. He devoted all his waking hours tracking Jeff's movements beginning with the night when Jeff abandoned Barbara. Through Jeff's place of employment, Larry discovered that Jeff had moved to

Philadelphia. He traced him from there to the Green Rock Resort. When he learned from an employee at the resort that Jeff had moved to Brussels, Larry pursued him, tracking him down, following him from his workout at the health club to the break-in at the Atomium on that fateful evening. It wasn't only the terror of his brother-in-law firing that gun at him. What tortured Jeff every night was also his suppressed guilt about Barbara's death.

Jeff folded his arms on the table, waiting for Leopold's reaction.

"Absolutely astounding," Leopold whispered. "So, … he followed you to the Atomium?"

"Well, I had just turned around on the landing from removing that cigarette case, and there the fucker was—standing at the bottom of the stairway—pointing a gun directly at me. I screamed at him. I don't know what the hell I said, but it sure didn't help. He started shooting, missing me at first, but the third shot hit me in my chest, directly over my heart. It went no further, stopped by that pewter case—it saved my life!"

All the pieces of evidence from the case file began forming a clear mosaic for Leopold.

"What about Larry? What happened?" Leopold asked.

"The shot to my chest knocked me flat on my ass. I don't know how long I was out, but when I came to, the next thing I knew, I was gazing down those steel steps at the bloody scene below. I struggled to my feet, stumbled down the stairs, hopped across that gory mess, and got the hell out of there as fast as my wobbly legs would carry me."

Sensing he was about to close the case that had been taunting him for twenty-five years, Leopold leaned back in his chair, fought off a victorious grin and exhaled his reply. "Such a dreadful story, Jeff … Now I understand why that dramatic incident in the dressing room last night upset you so much. Thank you for trusting me with your tragic story. I'm delighted to be able to return your grandfather's gift to you."

"It's like having part of him back. I should be the one thanking you. Hey, you haven't even touched your cheese Danish, my friend."

Leopold laughed. "No appetite now. The excitement of this discussion has left me sated!"

They stood up and shook hands. Jeff walked Leopold to the exit.

"If you're ever in Philadelphia, Leopold, please look us up … you know my name!"

Leopold embraced him. "You know I will, my friend!"

Jeff stood in the lobby, squeezing the penknife in his hand. Opening his palm, he fixed his gaze upon it, as if reclaiming part of his lost soul. He was as close to praying as he had ever been since his days in the seminary decades earlier. "God bless you, Grandpa," he uttered softly, as if just absolved from his sin.

Back in their hotel room, Margie was pacing. *Where the devil is he? We're gonna be late again!* Then she heard the keycard slide into the lock on the door. "Finally! Well, honey, what was that all about?"

"Margie, it's like some weird miracle. When I was living here with your dad and Heinrich, somewhere along the line I lost a gift my grandfather had given me on my graduation day from high school." Jeff opened his palm again. "It was this penknife."

Margie was immediately taken with its pearl handle—and the *CJL* initials. "How gorgeous! And the initials seem so eerie in a way."

"It's uncanny, for sure," Jeff said. "It's like an omen or something."

"But how did Leopold ever trace this magnificent knife to you—where did he ever get it?"

"Mr. Beckers is a retired police detective. He found it way back when I was living here. And get this: He attended CJ's concert in New York, and when he saw his name in the program, those initials—*CJL*—just rang a bell or something. Then the concert last night—well that clinched it for him. It seems that somehow—and I don't want to sound crazy—my grandfather wanted me to get it back. I can hardly wait to give it to CJ. He's gonna flip out when I tell him all about it."

Margie embraced Jeff, kissing him more passionately than she ever had since their honeymoon. "I can't tell you how wonderful it feels to see you so happy."

Jeff slipped the knife into his pocket, closed his eyes and hugged her. *Am I finally free from the torture that's been plaguing me all these years?*

※

Across town, Leopold settled into his seat on the train, contemplating Jeff's early morning revelations. Gazing out the window, he recalled Arthur telling him that Heinrich Winterbottom had sold Laurence the Mozart Requiem fragment concealed in a damaged cigarette case. Now he knew it was Jeff who retrieved the case from the Atomium. The penknife was returned to Jeff. The story was finally completed.

# Chapter 28

Christopher, Margie, and Jeff spotted Matt and Leo at the concierge desk as soon as they got off the elevator. Still giddy from the early morning revelation, Jeff bellowed across the lobby. "Look out everybody, the dynamic duo has arrived! No one's safe now."

His two adopted brothers swiveled around and rushed across the lobby.

"Ah! There he is—the toast of Brussels! How's it going, CJ?"

"A bit worn around the edges, Matt, but I think I'll survive."

"You look damned good to me, kid."

"So, where are we headed now, Captain Marvel?" Jeff asked.

"See that shiny black banana boat out there?" Matt answered, pointing to the stretch limousine in the driveway in front of the hotel. "It's ready to take us on a voyage to the most fab building in Brussels, where we're gonna sit on top of the world for our luncheon celebration."

"Don't you two ever stop partying?" Jeff asked. "All right, where is this architectural masterpiece?"

Leo pointed to the massive mural on the wall of the lobby.

"See that spectacular building in the center of that mural—with the shiny, silver globes—like some kind of magical Ferris wheel?"

Jeff's proud-father demeanor suddenly devolved to that of a terrified, cornered child. *I can't go back there again,* he thought, focusing on the target of Leo's index finger: an image of the Atomium.

"Are you all right, dad?" Christopher asked, ... receiving no response.

"Hey, folks, if this is all too much after last night's festivities, we totally understand," Leo said, following a glance at Matt. We'll cancel our get-together so you can rest a bit and—"

"No," Jeff interrupted. "Sorry, everyone, I think the alcohol level has finally destroyed any remaining grey matter in my brain. Of course, we'd be delighted to join you."

"That's our Jeff, now! Okay, then, folks. Our chariot awaits us," Matt announced.

Twenty minutes later the limo entered the grounds of the fabled architectural artifact at the Brussels World Fair. Everyone in the car was thrilled at seeing the building's glittering steel globes dominating the countryside—everyone except Jeff. For the second time that day, memories of that dark night decades earlier tore through his mind: the image of his brother-in-law aiming a gun at him, the bloody aftermath, and the overwhelming feeling of guilt about the death of his ex-wife.

"Relax, honey," Margie whispered, taking hold of his hand. "We'll have a nice lunch and get back to the hotel for a nap."

Jeff managed a faint smile.

Soon all were standing before the towering, improbable assemblage of steel globes. Matt pointed to the sphere at the very top of the structure. "That's where we'll all be in a few seconds—eating lunch high in the sky!" he said.

"It's got the most magnificent view of the city," Leo added.

Inside the Atomium, Jeff froze, glowering at the long steel stairway leading up to the first globe. He grasped his chest where the cigarette case had stopped a bullet decades earlier. A sharp pain suddenly stabbed the left side of his head. He squinted at the dull grey space at the bottom of the stairs where his brother-in-law's body had slumped to the floor, splattered in blood. Jeff grasped his aching head with both hands, Larry's words piercing his brain. *You murdered my sister, and now I'm gonna execute you!*—words dooming Jeff to an eternity of nightmares. He stumbled forward and collapsed, his head slamming against the concrete floor, fatefully near the very spot where Larry Ingles had uttered them.

# Chapter 29

Within five minutes a team of medics were huddled around Jeff Lambert's body, frantically trying to resuscitate him. One was rapidly performing compressions against Jeff's chest as another applied a Bag Valve Mask to stimulate ventilation. The chief medic was studying Jeff's face: lips already blue, eyes wide open and motionless. "Get him to AKH! He's got to be intubated!"

The crew scrambled to get Jeff into the ambulance. As it sped away, a guide from the Atomium staff approached Margie. "They're taking him to Vienna General, Mrs. Lambert. It's the university hospital. They'll take diligent care of him." Margie just stared. The guide scribbled a note to Christopher. "Here's the directions."

Christopher glanced at the piece of paper and turned, dazed, to Matt and Leo.

"Let's get you and your mom to the hospital right away," Leo said, slipping the directions out of Christopher's trembling hand. Minutes later they were speeding toward the Allegmeines Krankhaus der Stadt, the city's university hospital.

Inside the E.R., Leo asked about Jeff's condition.

"They're attending to Mr. Lambert now," the admissions nurse said. "He's not yet regained consciousness. You can all wait in the small conference room across the hall until the doctor has completed his evaluation of Mr. Lambert's condition. He'll meet with you there."

Inside the conference room, Margie began sobbing uncontrollably.

Christopher tried comforting her, to no avail. Wrapped in her son's arms, she sobbed: "Your dad was the happiest I've seen him in many years—maybe ever! It's impossible this could happen to him.

He hasn't been sick, and you know how he's always exercising or running and all. *It makes no sense.*"

A young doctor entered the room, accompanied by a nurse. "Mrs. Lambert?"

"Yes, doctor. I'm Margaret Lambert, and this is my son, Christopher."

All were on their feet as the doctor approached Margie. Looking down at his iPad, then back at her and Christopher, he cleared his throat and began.

"Mrs. Lambert, I'm Doctor Geierhaas. I'm terribly sorry to tell you that your husband suffered a major hemorrhagic stroke. A small artery, causing rapid bleeding in his brain. Unfortunately, he never regained consciousness. There was nothing we could do to save him."

"How could this happen!" she screamed.

"Well, Mrs. Lambert, we discovered that your husband had been taking one hundred milligrams of Lisinopril daily. That's quite a high dosage of medication for hypertension. This kind of—"

"*Hypertension?* I'm a nurse, and except for his nightmares I've never seen any symptoms of that. He never said anything to me about hypertension. ... Did you know anything about this, CJ?"

"No. I just can't believe it, mom. I never saw him taking any meds at all."

"He had a small container of Lisinopril in his jacket pocket, Mrs. Lambert," the doctor continued. "Has he been under any unusual pressure lately?"

"He's had ... terrifying nightmares for almost as long as we've been married—24 years. He'd wake up in the middle of the night, terrified, but never say anything about it. I begged him to get help, but he always brushed it off."

"Mrs. Lambert, that kind of anxiety may account for his need for such a high dosage of hypertension medication—and may explain the cause of the ruptured artery. The extensive period that you mentioned within which he has suffered those nightmares could certainly have contributed to his condition. Sometimes a sudden shock can trigger the onset of this kind of hemorrhage."

Margie, sitting back down, put her elbows on her knees and cradled her head in her hands. "I can't believe he's gone!" she wept.

"You may see your husband now," Dr. Geierhaas offered.

"Yes, I want to see him right away, please." Christopher helped her to her feet. "CJ, Matt, Leo, let's all of us go see him."

On a gurney in the triage room, a white blanket covered Jeff up to his neck. His face was pale blue, his lips purple, his mouth slightly open. Margie approached the body, tears dropping onto her husband's face. She leaned forward and kissed him. "Why didn't you let me know you were feeling so upset all the time, honey?" she whispered. "Maybe I could have …" She rested her head on his chest and closed her eyes.

Matt and Leo embraced Christopher.

The next morning, Leopold Beckers was sipping coffee at the kitchen table as Linn prepared breakfast. Opening the morning's paper, he turned to the regional news. The headline *"Tragedie in het Atomium"* captured his attention. He rose from his chair after reading the opening paragraph.

"What is it, dad? Are you okay? What's happening?"

"I can't believe it! Read this story. It's about Jeff Lambert. He's dead!"

Linn skimmed through the report, her jaw dropping as she envisioned Jeff and his family. "Dad, they were so happy the night before—and now this!"

"We've got to help them, Linn. They'll have to contact the American Embassy to arrange transportation of his body back to the states. They must feel terribly lost, Linn. How about calling them at the Hilton and offering our help?"

"Of course, dad. Give them a few hours. I am sure they're exhausted. We'll have a quick breakfast and get ready. I'll call them."

At ten o'clock that morning, Linn was on the phone with Christopher. "This is Linn Beckers. I'm so sorry about your father. My dad and I met you after the concert at—"

"Yes, of course I remember you, Linn," Christopher replied.

"My father saw the story in the morning paper. We're shocked.

"Who is it, CJ?" Margie asked.

"Mom, it's the lady who stopped backstage the other night with her father. You know—the detective who had coffee with dad the day he—"

Margie took the phone from him.

"Hi, this is Margie. Thank you for calling. Jeff was delighted after he spoke with your father the other day. They really seem to have hit it off." She began crying.

"Is there anything I can do to help?" Linn asked.

"I don't know what's going to happen," Margie replied. "Everything's so upended right now."

"Mrs. Lambert, my dad is quite familiar with the laws and protocol in situations like this. He would be glad to help with arranging for the return of your husband to the states, ... whenever you're prepared to proceed."

Margie was silent for a moment. "I haven't even thought about that! Yes, of course, that would be quite helpful. I just don't know what to do next."

"My father knows, so don't worry. Here is our cellphone number."

"Oh ... Linn ... could you please give that to CJ. I just can't concentrate. Here he is, and thank you ever so much for reaching out to us."

# Chapter 30

On Friday morning, Linn and her father accompanied Christopher and Margie to the American Embassy after helping them obtain an affidavit attesting to the contents of the casket and the Transfer Permit from the funeral director in Brussels who had received Jeff's body. Margie and Christopher decided to cremate Jeff's body as he had often stipulated to Margie. Then they contacted the airline to change the flight dates and arrange for their return home.

"Please join us for lunch," Margie said. "I'm sure Matt and Leo would be delighted to see you both again before we all leave. I just want to tell you how much we appreciate your helping us with everything, Mr. Beckers. And thank you, too, Linn. I can't imagine what we would have done. You know, Jeff was so uplifted after having coffee with you the other day, inspector."

"No 'inspector' anymore!" Leopold objected. "Remember, I'm retired."

"Does he really *sound* like he's retired?" Linn asked, jokingly.

"Not at all!" Margie said. "But I *am* curious, Mr. Beckers, about what you and my husband discussed. I'd love to hear about it over lunch."

Leopold was silent. "Dad?" Linn poked him. "What do you say, dad?"

"Oh, sorry for the momentary lapse. I was just thinking about that conversation. Of course, I'd be glad to discuss it with you at lunch."

※

"Thanks so much for inviting us," Linn said, as she and Leopold joined Margie and Christopher in the hotel dining room for lunch.

"You've been so exceedingly kind to us, Margie replied. "You're almost like family at this point."

Matt approached a minute later. "Hey folks, so good to be with you again." He shook Leopold's hand and pecked Linn on the cheek. Leo was right behind him.

"Margie and CJ told us how much you've helped them," Leo said. "We're truly glad we all got to meet one another."

"I'm happy we could help," Leopold replied, as they took their seats at the table. "You know, Christopher, I was moved by the love your father had for you. He was terribly proud of your accomplishments at such an early age. I mean, here you are—not yet twenty-four years old—and you're performing at some of the great concert halls in Europe."

"I loved him so much," Christopher said.

"Remember, son, as your career begins to flourish—think about your dad and how awfully proud he would be," Leopold added. "He will inspire you to greatness. I'm sure."

"What a lovely thought, Leopold. Thank you," Christopher replied.

Margie stared at Christopher, her eyes burning as she held back tears seeing the lost look on her son's face. "Leopold, may I ask what it was about your conversation with Jeff that excited him so much? It certainly lifted his spirits higher than they'd been in years."

"It's quite a long story, Margie. But when Jeff saw that penknife his grandfather had given him, it transformed his entire mood. Jeff was somehow reunited with him."

"You know, that's exactly what Jeff told me when he got back to our room. But how could such an incredible coincidence have happened? Twenty-five years ago, he lost the knife, and here you are—somehow finding him. It's all so mysterious to me." Margie's voice was beginning to crack. "And now ... he's gone." She pulled s handkerchief out of her purse and blotted her eyes.

"It's like it was just meant to be," Matt said. "Somehow that penknife had to get back to CJ."

"I've seen things like this happen during my career with the police department," Leopold said. "It's odd how a variety of circumstances can somehow have a way of connecting in the strangest way. For instance, your brother, Heinrich, had come to Brussels to get breakthrough medical treatment for your father. Jeff was employed by him, so he went with them as your dad's physical therapist. But while they were here in Brussels, your brother asked Jeff to go to the Atomium to retrieve some sort of missing heirloom that Heinrich had been told was hidden there."

"Now *that* is truly mysterious," Matt said.

Smiling for the first time in two days, Margie sighed. "That's just like Jeff—Indiana Jones at the Atomium in search of a lost treasure!"

For a moment, everyone enjoyed the turn in mood.

Leopold resumed his account. "It turns out that the heirloom is that very cigarette case unveiled by Christopher after his spectacular concert the other night. That's why Jeff reacted in such a shocked and disruptive way. When he saw it, the entire episode that had haunted him for so long suddenly erupted."

Margie gasped in disbelief. "But inspector—uh, sorry—Leopold, why would such a simple errand as that cause Jeff nightmares? You should've seen the way he awakened in terror."

"Ah, yes, but that's not all." Leopold went to describe the confrontation, and subsequent tragedy, that occurred that evening between Jeff and his former brother-in-law inside the Atomium.

"No wonder he was so terrified all these years! If only he had told me about it! Maybe we could have gotten him into therapy or something that might have provided some relief."

"It's okay, mom. We're gonna be all right," Christopher assured her.

"As horrible as this insane saga's been," she sighed, "somehow it's helping to bring closure to those monstrous nights that consumed so much of Jeff's life. Now I have an idea what he must have been going through—and I know *why*. If only I could have helped him."

"You *did* help him, mom. Regardless of the nightmares and all, you were there for him whenever he needed you. I'll always remember the love the two of you shared."

"And dad loved you so much, CJ." Margie turned to the others. "I want to thank you for all you've done for us. I know you've got a lot to do, so I don't want to delay you."

"My dad and I will continue to help you in any way we can. Just call us," Linn replied. "I'll be flying back to New York tomorrow afternoon."

"We're leaving tomorrow, too," Margie said. "Matt and Leo have made all the arrangements. Thanks, again."

"Hey, the credit goes to Wolfgang Amadeus Mozart," Leopold responded. "If it hadn't been for that Mostly Mozart concert in New York, we might never have met."

"Mozart's the ultimate gift that keeps on giving!" Christopher quipped.

*If this young man only knew how true his words really are,* Leopold thought, as all headed for the lobby.

# Chapter 31

The Austrian Federal Police cordoned off the black Mercedes-Benz crash site, while the forensics team photographed the tire tracks leading west on Kasernenstrasse along the airport perimeter and dusted the interior of the vehicle for fingerprints. The medical examiner supervised the removal of the bodies from the wreckage.

"They picked this baby clean," Lieutenant Wiesner said. "Even the victims' shoes and clothes."

The detective searching the back seat of the vehicle heard a low, pulsing sound. Lowering his head close to the floor, he traced the tone to the track under the front passenger seat. Training his flashlight on the area, he spotted the black plastic edge of Oliver Yates's cellphone. Sliding his thumb and index finger along the track, the detective nudged the phone loose. It fell to the floor. He seized it and pressed the response icon. Oliver Yates's name flashed on the small screen.

"Lieutenant, this phone belonged to a 'Mr. Yates,'" the detective said, holding the phone up as he spoke. "Unfortunately, the battery went dead right afterwards."

The lieutenant walked to the car. "Still got your magic touch, I see, Detective Tottser. Get it to the lab for analysis."

Three hours later, the gypsy gang rolled into a field at the eastern section of Vienna where they had set up a village bazaar near an amusement park. The gang drove around the back of the market to a large tent, slammed on the brakes of the old Citroen, unloaded their stolen cargo, then sped off to their next rendezvous.

Lavinia, a middle-aged gypsy who fled to Vienna with her family from Russia four decades earlier, sorted through the latest mound of plunder, distributing items to the other women to prepare them for sale. Her father, Alfonso Lakatos, the camp leader, had appointed her manager of the merchant operation because of her dominant personality and management skills.

"Good work!" Lavinia called out to her helpers as they rummaged through the pile. "We have cellphones!" Her daughters raised their heads from the loot, but quickly returned to their jobs readying the merchandise for the weekend bazaar. "Ah! Papa will like this—two guns!" she added. After checking the chambers and removing the bullets, she took the Glock19 and SIG P226 9 mm to her father's office.

"Look at this beautiful coat, mama!" her youngest daughter, Mahala, called out as Lavinia was passing by her table. She was holding up the navy-blue sport coat that hours earlier had been torn from the final embrace of Oliver Yates's lifeless body.

Lavinia took the jacket and, seeing the Burberry label inside, said, "Ah, we get good price! Quickly, press good and put on hanger. Students will be coming."

# Chapter 32

"**H**ey, guys, let's stop at the gypsy bazaar and see what's going on there this weekend," Kent Niessen said to his friends as they drove away from the amusement park toward the center of Vienna. It was a favorite way for the foursome to cap off a fun afternoon, especially today, when Kent learned he was chosen to receive a final interview for admission to the University of Music and the Performing Arts. Being selected for a face-to-face meeting with officials of the famed music school was tantamount to one's acceptance and a full scholarship.

"You're a genius, Kentmeister," said Gretchen, Kent's latest steady girlfriend, seated next to him in the front seat. She reached over and squeezed his hand. "You're gonna knock 'em dead with that sexy tenor voice of yours."

"Take it easy, Gretch!" Markus Osterle, Kent's best friend, who had grown up with him in Vienna, admonished. "We know our Kent's going to shine brighter than the other three thousand students at the University. But we can't let it go to his already big head."

Kent smirked into the rearview mirror. "I know *you* certainly won't let that happen."

They laughed as Kent steered his decade-old, blue Volkswagen Jetta into the unpaved parking area adjacent to a dozen tents where gypsies were hard at work hawking their most recently acquired merchandise. Markus's friend Brad, scanning the displays laid out before them, was the first to comment once all four were out of the car. "It looks like they're pretty well-stocked this week," he said,

151

approaching a cluster of tables—sporting a variety of clothing, housewares, electronics, paintings, and sculptures.

Gretchen and Brad made a beeline to a tent displaying racks of artwork, while Kent and Markus approached a tent where all sorts of clothing hung from metal racks.

"Maybe I can find something presentable to wear for my interview tomorrow," Kent said. "My threads are wearing a bit thin."

"My friend, your threads have been wearing thin since our first year in high school," Markus said. "I can't remember you buying any clothes since you moved in with me four years ago."

"I'm sure glad we're the same size!"

They strolled through two other tents before arriving at one with a large table stacked high with shirts, belts, trousers and shoes. Kent began pawing through a row of garments hanging from the tent's frame, stopping only at a blue sport coat near the end of the rack. Ten seconds later, Kent, wearing Oliver Yates's final birthday gift, was gazing into a cracked mirror propped against a pole in the rear of the tent.

"Look, Markus. It's a Burberry!"

"Wowza! What a bonanza, old buddy. And it seems to fit you."

"Like a glove, Markus. It's like it was tailor-made for me." He turned to the young woman behind the table. "How much is it?"

"Very expensive coat, sir. This is fine fabric. We must sell for seventy-five Euros—no less."

"What?" Kent exclaimed, removing the jacket and dropping it onto the table. "That's highway robbery!"

An older woman approached from behind the clerk, frowning.

"These boys make problem, Mahala?" Lavinia said.

Kent held up his right hand. "Hey, no problem! I'm a student, so I can't afford to pay that much. That's all."

"Whatcha can afford, young man?" Lavinia asked. "This is very handsome jacket, no?"

Kent looked at Markus, then directly back at Lavinia. "It sure is, ma'am, but I've only got twenty-five Euros to spend today. I'm sorry." He started to walk away.

"Wait, wait, okay. You give me fifty and coat is yours."

Kent pulled a bunch of Euros out of his pocket, counted them slowly, handed them to her, and picked up the sport coat. "Thank you, ma'am. I really appreciate it."

"Yeah! You 'appreciate'—and I go broke!"

Kent placed the jacket over his arm, and the two sauntered away in search of Brad and Gretchen.

"You should switch your area of graduate studies from voice to acting, Kent. You sure pulled the wool over that old dame's eyes! It was quite dramatic!"

"Bullshit! You know damned well it was fifty Euros she wanted all along."

They laughed, then Markus spotted Gretchen two tents away, holding up a framed canvas to Brad, one clearly too big to ever fit in the small Jetta. They walked over to them.

"Hey, let me see that. Nice color, Kent!" Gretchen said, as she placed the canvas back on the table. "It's gonna go really great with your deep blue eyes."

"Babe, you're not gonna believe how great it fits." He slipped it on, modeling it for his friends as if on a Gucci runway. His athletic 6'-2" physique and sculpted chest fit the fantasy.

Gretchen stopped him in his tracks, kissing him.

"You look so damned sexy in that coat, Kent. I just wanna hug you."

"Wait 'til I get the jacket off, okay! I don't wanna mess it up before my interview on Tuesday." He handed the coat to Markus. Kent and Gretchen fell into a deep embrace.

"Come on, guys! Let's not draw a crowd," Brad chided.

Kent and Gretchen halted their smooching.

"We'll continue this when we get home," Kent whispered in her ear.

She rubbed her groin against Kent's erect reaction to her embrace. They slowly slipped apart, Kent grabbing the coat from Markus, draping it in front of him.

"Mmm, I can hardly wait!" Gretchen murmured.

※

"I'm *in*, buddy!" Kent said, as soon as he heard Markus's voice on the phone Friday afternoon. "It took me two-and-a-half hours with three professors—but I did it! I got the notice today."

"Damn, Kent! It was that magic blue coat you swindled from those gypsies that put you over the top, dude."

"Maybe you're right, but on the way home from the university I got the hem of the jacket caught in the door jamb of my VW and ripped it," Kent replied. "I'm afraid I jinxed my good luck charm."

"Not to worry. I know the perfect person to bring that coat back to its prime condition," Markus said.

"Are you kidding me? It's just an old coat."

"No 'just' about it! That coat's a keepsake, and I'm gonna take it to Andreas Shankowitsch. He's my dad's friend and the best master tailor in Vienna. He'll fix it flawlessly. It's my gift to you to celebrate your new status as a student at the University of Music and the Performing Arts."

"No debate—I'll give it to you tonight!"

# Chapter 33

Andreas Joseph Shankowitsch was the fifth generation of tailors to ply his trade in the center of Vienna, in the same shop his family had run since the early 19<sup>th</sup> century. Sought out by members of the Vienna Philharmonic since the early '70s, he also resolved scores of sartorial emergencies for guest soloists at the Musikverein. His third great-grandfather had once fitted Ludwig von Beethoven's formal attire for a performance in the city. Although a bit eccentric, the aging tailor toiled as much as ten hours each day in his shop—classical music blaring from the massive Klipsch speakers he had installed decades earlier.

"Are there any recordings *other than* Mozart in your collection?" his clients often moaned as he fitted them for new outfits or for those they had outgrown. But the complaints were mostly in jest, for everyone knew Andreas worshipped the great composer. "Ach!" he'd say. "Why should I waste my precious time listening to the works of all the runners-up? And besides, Maestro Mozart once lived just down the street from this very shop."

Markus Osterle strolled across the Graben and turned onto Operngasse. Halfway down the block he spotted the foot-high, faded gold-leaf lettering—SHANKOWITSCH—on a wooden slab suspended from a bar jutting out from a storefront. The tailor shop was sandwiched between a pharmacy and a jeweler. Markus pushed open the warped wooden door, a loud bell clanging over it as he entered. He approached the counter meekly, awaiting the revered tailor's appearance from behind the bright red curtain separating the common folk from the sanctuary behind it. *Don Giovanni* was blaring so loudly from the back of the shop that Markus wondered if the old man could even hear the bell. An off-key but robust accompaniment to the opera's *"Notte E Giorno Faticar"* aria, which he assumed was that of Andreas himself, bemused Markus. Half a minute passed before a diminutive old man, with bushy white hair and a matching three-inch wide mustache, pushed back the curtain, seemingly annoyed by the interruption of the aria.

"What is it, young man?" he asked, having shuffled his way to the counter.

Surprised by Andreas's slight physical appearance, incongruous with the *basso profundo* voice he had just heard, Markus managed only a weak smile in response—unreciprocated by the aged baritone.

"Good morning, sir," he finally said, extending the coat to Andreas. "A friend of mine had a slight accident, ripping the hem and back of this coat. I want to get it fixed for him as a gift, so I came to the best tailor in Vienna."

Momentarily appeased by the young man's adulation, the tailor smiled slightly as he took the jacket in his hands and examined it, silently.

"My friend has a great tenor voice and has just been accepted to study vocal arts at the University," Markus went on, apologetically. "He wore this jacket for his final acceptance interview. It's a Burberry, sir."

"Yes, a Burberry. Do you think you're impressing me? A Burberry! Have you seen the coats *I've* created right here in this shop?"

Markus took a step back.

"Yes, sir, I have. You made my father's wedding tuxedo—and my First Holy Communion suit."

Andreas positioned the Burberry on the counter with the back of the coat face-up. Twirling his trembling arthritic index finger, he pointed to Markus. "Of course! You are Wilhelm Osterle's boy!"

"Amazing, sir! How did you—"

"I never forget a customer's face! You are Wilhelm's spitting image."

Andreas turned his attention back to the torn hem and panel. "Yes. I will fix it for you, and it will look better than Burberry ever could have made it."

"Thank you, Herr Shankowitsch. My friend will be truly delighted."

"Of course, he will! You can stop by next Thursday to pick it up—one hundred Euros."

"One *hundred* …?"

"Yes, yes, all right. Since your father is already a customer, I'll do it for eighty."

"Fine, Herr Shankowitsch. Thank you."

"You can pay me when you come back, young man," Andreas said, as he scratched *100* off the receipt, replacing it with *80*. "Oh, and next time bring your tenor friend. We can sing a powerful Don Giovanni and Commendatore duet together!"

In a sweeping, theatrical movement, the old tailor raised his right arm, and disappeared through the curtain, returning to his role as baritone in the first act of his favorite opera.

"Papa, you're not going to believe who I met yesterday," Markus said to his father, over morning coffee at their favorite café on the Kohlmarkt.

"So now I'm a *mind reader*?"

Markus laughed. For years, since moving into his own apartment, he looked forward to Saturday mornings with his dad.

"Come on, papa, take a guess. Who did I meet?"

"Okay, let's see … Sebastian Kurz!"

"Why would I meet the Chancellor of Austria?" Markus chuckled.

"You could do worse. You know they call him *wunderwuzzi*!"

"Not so sure about that, papa. He doesn't seem like a whiz kid to me! Okay, it was Herr Andreas Shankowitsch!" He announced the name as if talking about the chancellor himself.

"Hah! Is that old bugger still working? He must be a hundred years old!"

"Yes! I took Kent's new coat to have repaired. You should hear Herr Shankowitsch's voice—an unbelievably powerful baritone."

"Let me tell you something, son. That man's a living legend in Vienna. You wouldn't believe some of the clients he and his family have served."

"You know what, papa? He actually recognized my face, and before I could identify myself, he uttered your name."

"The old boy's still with it, I guess. I must stop by the shop sometime to see him."

"Yeah, he'd probably like that. I mentioned to him that he made your wedding tuxedo."

"He sure did, son. And it cost me a bundle! I'm saving that tux for *your* wedding."

"I guess we'll have to give it to Andreas," Markus replied. "It's going to need a lot of cutting and resizing."

"I'm afraid so, son. Only Herr Shankowitsch will be able to pull off such a miracle!"

# Chapter 34

On Monday, working late into the night, Andreas scanned the variety of garments hanging on the repair rack in his shop. He took down the blue jacket, smiling at the memory of Wilhelm Osterle's wedding and his young son's Holy Communion. Spreading the Burberry coat on a large metal worktable, he hunched over, studying its torn back panel and hem. Turning away from it briefly, he increased the volume on the final movement of Mozart's Jupiter Symphony, the composer's final masterpiece of that genre, waving an imaginary baton in sync with its miraculous quintuple invertible counterpoint finale. With a flourish he turned off the player and got back to work.

Andreas ran his fingers along the edge of the hem, detecting a rigid section about two inches from the end. Lifting the jacket closer to his eyes he saw an oblong impression inside the hem. *Was ist das?* A small safety pin held the flaps of the hem together.

He removed the pin and, with a long tweezers from the drawer in the side of the table, Andreas carefully inserted the point of the tweezers. "Got it!" He pulled it gently toward the opening of the hem, as if defusing a live explosive device.

Five seconds later, an acrylic sleeve reflected the fluorescent light. Still grasping the tweezers, Andreas squinted as he moved it away from the bright glare. Examining it closely revealed a yellowish fragment of blank parchment inside. He turned it over. Adjusting his bifocals, he enunciated aloud the words on the paper: "*quam olim* ...." He placed the acrylic sleeve back on the table with the same reverence that he placed the Sacred Host on his tongue every Sunday morning. *"Mein Gott in Himmel,"* he said, forming his hands in prayer.

The old tailor's thoughts flashed back to 1958, when his parents took him to World Expo '58 in Brussels. He remembered his father's excitement at seeing Mozart's Requiem Mass autograph manuscript displayed just a few feet away from him. His father, too, had been an avid devotee of classical music, especially that of the great Austrian composer. Indeed, for three generations his family had maintained a yearly subscription to the Vienna Philharmonic season. He recalled how the next day's newspapers and radio stations in Brussels—and around the world— carried repeated reports of the damage done to the manuscript. His father's ecstasy had immediately turned to outrage.

Indeed, until the present day, news reports and television commentaries occasionally carried stories about the mystery of the manuscript page—showing photographs of the bottom-right corner taken of it before it was mutilated. Andreas's father had removed one such photograph, from *Het Laatste Nieuws,* and framed it, placing it in the tailor shop on the wall over the desk still used by Andreas.

Mixed feelings of disbelief and anxiety overtook Andreas as he gazed at what he believed to be the very fragment that had been missing for more than six decades. "What should I do?" he muttered.

Andreas recalled his father's veritable prayer when telling his young son about the missing fragment: "The Requiem Mass begs God to deliver the departed souls from the lion's mouth. May God soon rescue this sacred fragment from the lion's mouth, too, and guide it safely back to its place in the original manuscript." *Of course!* Andreas thought. *I must contact the Austrian National Library first thing in the morning.* He hurried to the front of the shop, locked the door and pulled down the shade. Back in his workspace, he slid a short stepladder in front of the wood-paneled wall behind the table. Atop its three steps, he stretched his left arm upward and lifted a large wooden clock off its hook on the wall. He stepped down, placed the antique German timepiece on the table, and picked up the tweezers.

He stepped back onto the ladder and reached up to the space from where the clock had been removed. Andreas inserted the tip of the tweezers into the small hole of a hidden panel his great grandfather had fashioned, and pulled it open. He reached into the cubicle behind it, removed a six-inch-square, grey metal strongbox inside, then stepped down to his worktable, where he placed the box. Taking a ring of keys out of his pocket, he inserted the smallest one into the lock, and opened the box. He placed the precious relic inside, under a stack of twelve thousand euros he had secretly accumulated over the years, savings for a surprise retirement cruise with his wife.

Back atop the ladder, he reached up and returned what had now become a reliquary to its cubicle inside the wall, not unlike a priest returning the ciborium of consecrated wafers into the altar's golden tabernacle after Communion.

After closing the wood panel, Andreas stepped down, took the clock from the table and, back again on the ladder, stretched his arms to return the clock to its place on the wall. A dull pain shot along his left arm. Balancing himself against the wall, he breathed deeply for a moment before managing to set the clock back on its hook. Looking up at the dull, brass Roman numerals on the clock, he gripped his left arm.

*When great-grandfather Johann built that secret hiding place, he could never have imagined the treasure it would someday harbor. Your final words will be secure in there, Herr Mozart, until I reunite them with your masterpiece!*

The tailor's call to the national library early the next morning, requesting immediate help, frazzled the secretary, who, seeing Franz Beitzel entering the office, mimed the words for him to take the phone. Beitzel listened to the old tailor's astounding, if rambling, claim. *Could this old man really know what he's got? Am I going on another wild goose chase?* He cancelled all appointments for the day, telling the receptionist that he had to leave for a couple of hours. Then he raced to Shankowitsch's shop.

# Chapter 35

Franz Beitzel arrived at the tailor shop just before noon. Andreas was flushed and perspiring as he greeted him, vigorously shaking his hand until, politely but forcefully, the library director extricated it from the old tailor's grip.

"Good morning, Herr Beitzel. Thank you for coming on such short notice," Andreas began. "I'm sure you're a very busy man."

"Not at all, Herr Shankowitsch," Beitzel said, stepping into the shop. "That's quite a remarkable claim you made on the phone. As you can imagine, I'm most interested in examining the item you described."

"I don't think you'll be disappointed, Herr Beitzel. I've got it in my strongbox. Come, come, please. I'll get it for you."

Andreas locked the door, placed the 'closed' sign on the window, and led Beitzel to the back of the shop. He grunted as he slid the ladder from the table to the wall. He climbed up and stretched to unhook the clock. He handed it to Beitzel, who had come around the worktable, watching Andreas struggle as he climbed.

"Would you please put this on the table, Herr Beitzel—and, oh, hand me those tweezers?"

Beitzel did as asked. "Here you are, sir. *Are you okay?*"

"Just a bit winded," Andreas replied. He reached up and pried open the compartment in the wall. Reaching inside, he pulled out the metal strongbox, handed it down to Beitzel, then started down the ladder. As he turned around on the bottom step, he grew dizzy and lost his balance. Beitzel attempted to steady him, but Andreas, gasping for air, spun out of Beitzel's grip and crashed to the floor.

Hearing the voices of pedestrians passing by the shop, Beitzel glanced at his watch. "I've got to get out of here." Ignoring Andreas's condition, he placed the metal box onto the counter and tried to open it. *The fucking thing's locked!* He bent over Andreas, checking the old man's jugular. *No pulse!* He reached into Andreas's righthand pocket and pulled out his keys, quickly selecting the one small enough to fit the lock on the strongbox. The first thing he saw when he opened it was the stack of money, which he impulsively stuffed into his briefcase. Looking back into the box, he saw the fragment. "This is it—the Holy Grail! I've finally got it!"

Removing the wad of euros from his briefcase, Beitzel returned them to the metal box, placed the fragment under the money, closed the box and stuffed it into his briefcase. He glanced at Andreas's body, then turned and hurried to the front door. Seeing no one outside, he slipped away.

"Count von Strasser, this is Beitzel."

"Yes, Herr Beitzel, what *now*?"

The irritation in the count's voice, spurred by the memory of his aide's failure to complete the earlier mission, put Beitzel on the defensive.

"This time I've *got* it, sir!"

"Are you certain, Beitzel? Are you sure you have the authentic item?"

"For sure, sir. And I won't let it out of my sight."

"Excellent, Beitzel! Bring it to Salzburg right away. Do you understand? I mean, get the next plane out of there and contact me as soon as you've got the flight number and times. I'll meet you at the airport. *Do you understand, Beitzel? Have you got that? Is it clear? Get down here right now.*"

"I'm on my way, count!"

163

Agnes Fichter, a longtime customer, discovered Andreas' body later that afternoon when she passed by the shop, seeing the door to the tailor shop ajar and the "closed" sign hanging in the window. She nudged the door open and cautiously entered the shop, calling repeatedly without a response. Walking around the counter and into the back room, she found Andreas lying face down aside the ladder, his right arm outstretched, an antique clock lying next to it, its ticking second hand the only sound breaking the silence. "Help!" she screamed.

Several medics had arrived within minutes of the next-door jeweler's phone call and were tending to Andreas when two police officers entered the shop. They noticed that a small cash register on the counter was closed. Opening the drawer, the constable noted that it was intact, the euros inside arranged neatly. "This clock could have been up there, inspector," the constable said, pointing to the hook on the wooden wall. Stepping up the ladder, he ran a flashlight along the faded outline of the clock. Spotting the slightly ajar panel door in the wall, he reached up and, with his gloved right hand, pulled it open.

"Something may have been inside this hidden space, but whatever it was is gone. We may be looking at a robbery here, constable. Seal off this property right away and get the forensics team here. And take Frau Fichter over to the office for further questioning. She may recall some key details once she's recovered from the shock."

"Tragedy ends era of tailors to Beethoven and the Philharmonic"— so read the headline of *Wiener Zeitung*, Vienna's oldest daily newspaper, detailing how the sudden death of Andreas Joseph Shankowitsch had ended five generations of the celebrated family's sartorial excellence in the city.

# Chapter 36

Interpol had been monitoring Count von Strasser's communications for information about *Ein Volk*'s suspected plot against the upcoming Salzburg Festival. Online chatter during the previous two months had revealed the Neo-Nazi group's plan to smuggle a deadly nerve gas into the city days before the festival. On the day before Beitzel's call to von Strasser, in fact, Interpol had tracked the movement of the nerve gas from North Korea to Vienna. When the agency intercepted Beitzel's call to the count— proclaiming "I've got it sir!"— they interpreted his words as a signal to the count that Beitzel, whom Interpol had identified as a member of *Ein Volk*, had secured the Russian VX nerve agent. Available only on black markets in North Korea and Russia. it was the same lethal poison Saddam Hussein had used in the 1980s on the Kurdish people in Iraq, claiming 5,000 victims. Interpol had also intercepted Beitzel's other call to von Strasser that reported his plane's flight number and expected time of arrival at Salzburg International Airport. Austrian Federal Police were waiting for him there.

Before leaving for the airport, Beitzel placed the twelve thousand euros into the safe installed in his den for the rare books he occasionally purchased, his favorite being an autographed copy of a first edition of Nietzsche's *Thus Spoke Zarathustra*. He then opened his slim, black-leather business card case and removed all the cards, replacing them with the acrylic sleeve, which he placed inside a folded index card.

He zipped the case shut and slipped it into the inside pocket of his suit jacket. He packed his overnight bag and hailed a taxi to Vienna International Airport.

At 5:30 that afternoon, Franz Beitzel settled into his seat in the Austrian Airlines Boeing 767-300, imagining the glowing reception he would receive from Count von Strasser when he arrived and presented the elusive treasure to him.

Posted inside Terminal 1 of Salzburg International Airport, the dozen Austrian Federal Police detectives who were awaiting their arrival studied photos of Beitzel and von Strasser on their mobile phones, every few minutes glancing at the incoming flight data from Vienna. By the time the airline announced Beitzel's flight number, the detectives had already strategically closed the semicircle they had formed at various positions around the arrival gate. A backup squad held positions about twenty yards behind theirs.

Count von Strasser, accompanied by his top aide, Lukas Rieger, struggling to keep up with the count's rapid pace, entered Terminal 1, heading in the direction of the gate.

As soon as the "permission" image blinked on the screen in front of him, Franz Beitzel snapped open his seatbelt and sprang up from his aisle seat to attempt a quick exit from the plane. Before he could get even his left foot into the aisle, however, an obese elderly woman seated across from him had already stretched her leg into the aisle, forcing him to halt. The woman struggled out of her seat and gripped the seat in front of her, pulling herself upward, groaning as she rose ever so slowly. Gazing helplessly at the overhead compartment, she shifted her eyes toward Beitzel. "Would you kindly reach for that large blue bag up there, young man?" she asked.

Beitzel grimaced at first, but, forcing a smile, was in the aisle and pulling the bag out of the compartment. By the time the woman had steadied herself, her bulky handbag and luggage now in her possession, the seats in front of them had emptied, she and the dozens of passengers in front of her jamming the aisle all the way to the exit.

Beitzel shuffled along behind her, finally reaching the door of the plane, then slow-walked through the tunnel leading inside the airport. He entered the terminal behind the still lengthy line in front of him, and, standing at the top of the stairs, looked down into the arrival area, perusing the crowded terminal below. Five years of experience as a field investigator with the Criminal Police Office in Vienna alerted him instinctively to the dragnet unfolding below: several detectives closing in on the gate, and Count von Strasser in the distance, walking briskly behind them. *They're on to us! What am I gonna do?*

Beads of sweat were forming on his forehead. In front of him, still, was the old woman, her handbag hanging open on her arm. He reached inside his jacket, pulled out the business card case, and slipped it carefully into the bag, memorizing as he did so the name on the strip of tape looped around its shoulder strap: *Maria Stabler, Maria Stabler, Maria Stabler. Auf Wiedersehen, Frau Stabler!*

When Beitzel finally arrived at the bottom of the stairs, Special Agent Neil Lienhardt stepped out from the crowd, flashing his blue and silver badge. "Franz Beitzel, you are under arrest."

Carefully slipping the overnight bag from Beitzel's hand, the bomb squad's disposal specialist accompanying Lienhardt placed it into a four-foot square metal container, which he then locked and lifted onto a steel cart. Two police officers escorted the specialist as he quickly wheeled the cart out of the terminal.

"Why are they taking my bag?" Beitzel barked to the agent.

"*We* will ask the questions, Herr Beitzel. You're under arrest for suspicion of participating in a terrorist plot."

"This is insane!" Beitzel screamed. "*Terrorist plot?* That's absolute nonsense! I am the assistant director general of the Austrian National Library. I assure you, sir, that you're making a profoundly serious mistake!"

"We are quite aware who you are, Herr Beitzel. You will be taken to Polizeianhaltdezentrum in Salzburg. You can plead your case there."

Beitzel's face paled. He was silent. *Von Strasser better bail my ass out of this, or he's going down with me.*

Rieger and the count had gotten within ten yards of Beitzel when they first noticed six detectives closing in on him.

"We've got to get the hell out of here, Rieger," the count mumbled. "Turn around slowly and walk away from me. We'll meet at the car."

Rieger headed for the terminal's east exit, the count for the west. As they scurried toward the exits, the outer ring of the Federal Criminal Police squad encircled them, snaring them before they could escape.

In the windowless, battleship-grey Polizeianhaltdezentrum interrogation room, Lienhardt sat across from Beitzel at a metal table.

"This is your 'Letter of Rights,' Herr Beitzel," the special agent said, sliding the bureaucratic form across the table to Beitzel. "I suggest you sign it for your own good."

Beitzel, completely familiar with the form, signed it and shoved it back to Lienhardt. "I am well aware of my rights, Agent Lienhardt."

"Very good, then," Lienhardt replied, "We understand each other." Raising his voice a full octave, Lienhardt continued. "I will repeat, Herr Beitzel. We are detaining you under suspicion of taking part in an international terrorist plot. Do you understand me?"

"I demand to be released at once. You have no evidence that I have committed any crime at all."

"Herr Beitzel, you do not seem to understand that you are in serious trouble. You're in no position to make demands for anything."

Beitzel was silent, wondering where von Strasser was—and why the count hadn't gotten him released by now.

Lienhardt stood up and, leaning across the table, began shouting at him. "This is your only shot! Cooperate with us! We will make things quite uncomfortable for you if you don't!"

Beitzel jerked back in his chair, recoiling from the agent's outburst. *There is nothing I can do but go on the offensive. It's all I've got.* "I will *not* destroy my career because of this massive blunder you and your team have made here today," he said. "Show me proof of your claim. Why are you charging me as a terrorist? How could I be involved in any kind of treachery? I have influential friends and associates in government and in the media. I will see that this outrageously misguided action receives all the attention it demands!"

"You will have your day in court, sir. In the meantime, we believe you pose a threat to society, so we are going to hold you here for further interrogation."

Lienhardt got up, rammed his chair against the table, turned, and walked out of the room, slamming the door behind him. He proceeded to the basement and entered a holding cell midway down the corridor.

"So, you are Count Frederick von Strasser."

"And *you* are …?"

"I am Special Agent Neil Lienhardt, and on behalf of the Republic of Austria, I am charging you with plotting an international terrorist catastrophe to occur right here in Salzburg." He placed a government form in front of the count. "This is your 'Letter of Rights,' Count von Strasser. I suggest you sign it for your own protection."

"Special Agent Whoever," Von Strasser laughed scornfully, as he signed the document, "you have made the mistake of your life! Your career is about to be brought to an abrupt and ignominious end." He was snarling now. "You have no idea what I can do to you for putting me—and my associate, Lukas Rieger—through this shameful ordeal. And, by the way, where *is* Mr. Rieger?"

"I know exactly who you are and what you've been doing for the past two years. I can show you transcripts of conversations that place you and your organization at the center of a terrorist plot against this country."

Shocked to realize that this wasn't about the Mozart fragment, but that his plot against the festival had been discovered, von Strasser doubled down. "Special Agent Lienhardt, I am a retired colonel of the Austrian Army of the Second Republic. I have served my country honorably. I belong to no organization that seeks to harm my country. Your claim is absurd. Once again, I demand that you show me evidence of your charge—or release me immediately!"

"Your demand for evidence will be satisfied in a court of law," Lienhardt shot back. "You will answer to them. You're not going anywhere."

# Chapter 37

The next morning, as a prison guard was taking Franz Beitzel to an image-processing room on the floor below, they passed the cell holding Count von Strasser; its metal door had just swung open, and a police officer was leading the count out of the cell. When Beitzel saw his Neo-Nazi boss in handcuffs, arms behind his back, he panicked. Struggling to escape the scene, Beitzel tore away from the guard and crashed to the cement floor, his head smashing against the steel door of the adjacent holding cell. Blood ran from the back of his head.

"What have you done to this man!" Count von Strasser cried out as the guard shoved the count back into his cell.

"Medic needed on lower level—now!" the guard barked into his radio.

Twenty minutes later, Beitzel lay unconscious on a small bed in the police department's infirmary, surrounded by a nurse, who was checking Beitzel's vital signs; the house physician; Special Agent Lienhardt, and the guard who had been escorting Beitzel.

"You've got to revive this man, doctor! He's a key witness."

"Agent Lienhardt, I'm not sure he's going to come out of this. He's unable to move his legs; and judging from the disjointed position of his neck when we found him, I suspect his spinal column may have been severely damaged, and—"

"How did this all this happen?" Lienhardt demanded, whipping his head around and addressing the guard.

"I was taking him down for processing when he saw von Strasser and totally freaked out, sir. When Beitzel bolted from my grip, he stumbled and fell against a cell door."

"You had orders to keep those rotten bastards separated! You've fucked up this entire case."

"Sorry, sir. Somehow, the detainees crossed paths, and I—"

"Get the hell out of my sight!"

Lienhardt turned back to the doctor. "What are his chances of regaining consciousness?"

"We'll know within the next hour or so. I suggest you stand by, Agent Lienhardt. He may lapse in and out if he comes to."

Meanwhile, Count von Strasser, back in his cell, was trying to figure out what happened to the Mozart fragment. *Where the hell is it? Have they recovered it? How could they have known about our plot for the festival? I've got to get out of here!*

Special Agent Lienhardt stood by as the doctor continued monitoring Beitzel's condition. Lienhardt's cellphone buzzed. It was the commander of the bomb squad's disposal unit. "We found nothing posing any danger in Beitzel's carry-on, nor anywhere in the clothes he was wearing. And he hadn't checked any luggage with the airline prior to boarding. *He's clean*, Agent Lienhardt."

"Where's the VX nerve gas?" Lienhardt mumbled. "We've lost the trail!"

※

Only ten minutes later, Beitzel began moving his lips.

"He's regaining consciousness, Agent Lienhardt."

Turning on his cellphone recorder, Lienhardt held it close to Beitzel's lips, poised for any words. Beitzel exhaled softly. The quivering became vigorous.

"What is it, Beitzel?" Lienhardt coaxed, pressing even closer. "What are you trying to say?"

Franz Beitzel was mumbling something before he slipped out of consciousness for the last time.

"Sta...Sta ... bler ... sta ... Ma... ri ... a...."

※

Finally in her room in the Altstadthotel Kasererbrau at mid-afternoon, following an exhausting day negotiating her way through two airport concourses, Maria Stabler slipped off her shoes and settled into a chair near the window. Situated at the foot of the Hohensalzburg Fortress, the old hotel had been a favorite of hers and her late husband, Dr. Peer Stabler. They had honeymooned there, in that very room, thirty-one years earlier. The Salzburg Festival had been their annual pilgrimage ever since. Now, however, Maria was there alone for the first time. *I miss you so much, Peer!*

Maria dozed off, awakening as dusk was settling over the old city, less than one kilometer from the home where Mozart was born. She got up from the chair, switched on the antique lamp next to it, and walked to the bed, where she had dropped her handbag upon arriving in her room. She opened the bag and extracted her copy of that morning's *Kronen Zeitung*, which featured a comprehensive story about the upcoming Festival. As she unfolded the newspaper, a small, black leather case fell to the floor.

Maria Stabler gazed at the unfamiliar object below her. *Was ist das?* She placed the newspaper on the bed, bent over and picked up the leather case, breathing heavily as she rose back up. Seated on the chair, she held the case under the lamp. She remained puzzled. *I've never seen this case before.* She unzipped it. Nothing inside but a folded white index card in one of the six slots. As she pulled out the card, an acrylic sleeve fell onto her lap. It contained a faded piece of blank parchment. She turned it over.

# Epilogue

A month after Leopold visited his daughter to celebrate his retirement—a celebration that turned out to encompass the two wildest weeks of his life—he returned to New York for the funeral of Laurence Kellerman. Ongoing anxiety over the loss of his most valuable and beloved possession had proved to be far too much for the 81-year-old attorney to bear. Cardiac arrest and multiple strokes ended his life.

Laurence bequeathed his entire estate and law firm to Arthur Keyes, whom Laurence loved as if he were his own son. Arthur rebranded the firm as Keyes & Beckers LLP.

Three months following Laurence's funeral, Linn called Leopold, telling him that she and Arthur were engaged to be married. A fall wedding was planned.

※

On November 4, 2015, as Leopold walked down the center aisle of St. Patrick's Cathedral, Linn holding his arm, the joy of the moment was colored by bittersweet memories. He couldn't help but recall the time he and his late wife had walked down that same aisle on their first visit to the famed cathedral.

"I love you so much, dad," his daughter whispered, seeing him dab an eye. "Thank you for everything you've done for me."

"I love you, too, honey. If only your mother were here. She'd be so incredibly proud of you."

The cardinal looked on as Leopold presented his daughter to Arthur Keyes.

As Leopold turned and walked to the pews, he spotted Margie and Christopher Jeffrey Lambert seated with Leo Weber and Matt Stephenson. Margie blew him a kiss, and her escorts waved back.

After the wedding ceremony, the guests gathered at the legendary Waldorf-Astoria Hotel for the festivities. Leopold greeted the central cast that comprised the melodrama of his retirement celebration earlier that year. "Margie and CJ, it's such a pleasure to see you both, especially under happy circumstances for a change. I hope you're both doing well. And Matt and Leo, it's good to be with you again."

"We're doing fine, Leopold. So good to be with you, too," Margie replied. "I've been promoted to superintendent of nursing at the University Hospital. I needed a challenge—and boy, did I ever get one!"

"And you, CJ?"

"I'm excited to tell you that in February I'm beginning a concert tour of four cities in the United States, first in Chicago, then in Philadelphia. I'd love it if you could visit. And more great news—Julie's been offered a position as principal violinist with the Philadelphia Orchestra. She's moving back to the city!"

"*Wunderbar!* I'm a frequent flier now. I would love to jet back here again. Just give me the date, and I'll be there. I'm looking forward to meeting Julie, too."

"That would be terrific, Leopold."

"And what about you two fellas?"

"Aloha, Leopold! Since the first of September, we've been ensconced in Waikiki Beach, soaking in every bit of what paradise has to offer," Leo replied. "And if you really want to rack up the miles, come on over!"

"Well, this old man may just take you up on that offer."

"We'll have a surfboard all waxed up and ready for you," Matt joked.

"Too much of a stretch for this worn-out detective!"

"Never count yourself out, detective," Leo replied. "You won't believe what a powerful influence this guy next to me can be.

Matt flashed the Hawaiian sign with his fingers. "Hang loose, Leopold. Hawaii brings peace and inspiration to the soul. Who knows what you might find yourself doing there?"

"We'll see what happens, my friends!" Leopold said. "Anything's possible, I guess!"

The next day, before Linn and Arthur left for their honeymoon cruise to the Mediterranean, they enjoyed a late lunch with Leopold at Oscar's, in the Waldorf-Astoria.

"Dad, are you sure you're going to be okay all alone in the big city?" Linn asked.

"Big city? Ha! I'm a crusty, old, retired detective who's been living all his life in what is now the capital of the European Union. Remember, the doctors gave me a clean bill of health. The tiny lump in my brain is gone! I'll be okay anywhere in the world, my dear. And I will be back home in a couple of days, so I can relax and enjoy the thought of my two favorite people in the world together at last."

"Leopold," Arthur replied, "Thanks for welcoming me into your family. I'm the luckiest guy on the planet right now."

In the predawn morning three days later, back home in Brussels, Leopold lay in bed, staring at the ceiling. *I could never have imagined the kind of year my retirement would bring. After all my concern about Linn's future, she found a partner in life. And I have finally closed the horrid case that hounded me for twenty-five years. And I became a character in the middle of a suspense thriller involving Wolfgang Amadeus Mozart himself.*

As morning sunlight drenched the room, the old detective sat on the edge of his bed, stretched his arms out wide, yawned, got up and walked to the window. He watched an airliner from the Brussels airport jetting into the sky. *Yates and Beitzel are dead, and von Strasser's rotting in prison. But where in God's name is that Requiem Mass fragment?*

His phone ringing so early in the morning startled Leopold. It was Karl Gerber, his friend from the Bundespolizei who had assisted Leopold at the very beginning of his involvement with Laurence's disappearance. "Leopold, you'd better come to Salzburg right away. I've just seen a report that Beitzel was spotted in an encounter with an elderly woman onboard his flight. The video surveillance shows that he slipped something into her handbag just before he entered the terminal."

*The fragment!* "I'll be in Salzburg tomorrow."

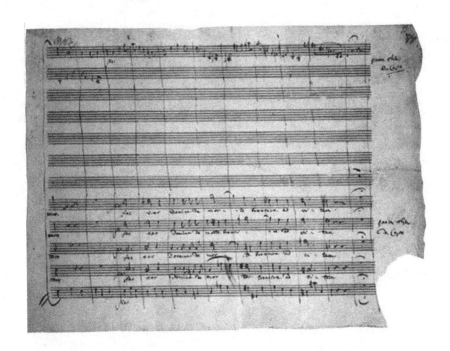

Pictured above is a photograph of the second-to-the-last page of the autograph manuscript of the Mozart Requiem in D Minor as it appears today, housed in the Austrian National Library in Vienna. The missing fragment—containing Mozart's last words—torn from the bottom right-hand corner of that page in 1958, has never been found.